CHEESIE MACK
MACK
IS SORT OF FREAKED OUT

READ ALL OF CHEESIE'S ADVENTURES!

CHEESIE MACK
IS SORT OF FREAKED OUT

STEVE COTLER

Illustrated by Douglas Holgate

random house 🏠 new york

Text copyright © 2014 by Stephen L. Cotler
Jacket art and interior illustrations copyright © 2014 by Douglas Holgate

"Standing on the Shoulders" by Lanny, Steve, and Doug Cotler. Published by Wail and Blubber Music, copyright © 1990.

Visit us on the Web! randomhouse.com/kids

Educators and librarians, for a variety of teaching tools, visit us at RHTeachersLibrarians.com

Library of Congress Cataloging-in-Publication Data
Cotler, Steve.
Cheesie Mack is sort of freaked out / Steve Cotler ; illustrated by Douglas Holgate.
—First edition.
pages cm.
Summary: "Cheesie and his best friend, Georgie, pull off a fantastic UFO prank, but when things go wrong, the victims of the prank plan a sinister plot as payback."
—Provided by publisher
ISBN 978-0-385-36988-6 (trade)—ISBN 978-0-385-36990-9 (ebook)
[1. Practical jokes—Fiction. 2. Halloween—Fiction. 3. Best friends—Fiction.
4. Friendship—Fiction. 5. Family life—Massachusetts—Fiction. 6. Middle schools—Fiction.
7. Schools—Fiction. 8. Massachusetts—Fiction.] I. Holgate, Douglas, illustrator. II. Title.
PZ7.C82862Chv 2014 [Fic]—dc23 2013039835

Printed in the United States of America

10 9 8 7 6 5 4 3 2 1

First Edition

Today my life is full of choice
Because a young man raised his voice
Because a young girl took a chance
I am freedom's inheritance
Years ago they crossed the sea
And they made a life for me
I'm standing on the shoulders
Of the ones who came before me

...for my grandparents

Contents

CHEESIE MACK
IS SORT OF FREAKED OUT

Chapter AAA

Not a Spoiler

My name is Ronald Mack. You can call me Cheesie. Everyone does.

This book tells all about my fifth adventure. Everything in this story really happened to me, and because I thought kids would like to read about it, I wrote it.

(I didn't exactly write *every* word of it because you'll see my friends contributed a little here and there.)

Granpa says some people start a new book by turning to the last page to see how the story ends. That seems goofy to me. A new book is like a mystery. You don't know how it's going to turn out, and every page is full of clues. So why spoil the mystery by looking ahead?

I mean, isn't it awful when a friend sees a movie before you do and then tells you what happened? That kind of don't-tell-me information is called a spoiler.

But what if you can't stand the suspense? What if you just have to know what happens?

I have come up with a compromise.

I'm going to tell you *some* of what happens. But I am *not* going to spoil the mystery by actually, specifically, and totally describing everything. It's more like I am going to give you some clues.

Here goes.

In this book you will find:

1. A large, four-legged reptile.
2. One of the witches from *The Wizard of Oz* (twice!).
3. An alien spacecraft.

4. Four pillowcases stuffed full of candy.

5. Flying rolls of toilet paper.

6. Buckets of brains and guts.

I put the above list in here for three reasons:

A. I like making lists.

B. I am hoping that you will say to yourself, "Wow! That list sounds super interesting. I hafta-gotta read this book!"

C. So that when I write *this* list, there will be two lists in a row, which I think is sort of funny.

In fact, I think it's so funny, here comes a third list in a row. It is entitled "Things I Would Like to Invent."

i. An alarm clock toaster so I could wake up to the smell of warm bread. (With a button to automatically peanut butter and/or jelly your toast.)

ii. A skateboard that would wind up a spring when you go downhill and unwind the spring to power you up hills. (Gloucester, my hometown, is absolutely not level.)

iii. Miniature cats the size of hamsters. (I told

this to my mom, and she said, "Oh, that would be so cute.")

iv. Barbecue sauce that's a color other than red or brown . . . maybe purple or blue. (Don't ask me why. . . . I just think the world needs it.)

v. What's your idea for an invention? If you have one, please go to my website and tell me what it is.

Okay. Enough lists.

My adventure starts on the next page. And I'm warning you . . . not everything in it is good for me.

I hope you like it. If you don't or do or whatever, please comment on my website and tell me why. (There's a whole list of website links at the back of this book. BUT DON'T PEEK AT THE ENDING!)

Ronald "Cheesie" Mack

Ronald "Cheesie" Mack (age 11 years and 4 months)

CheesieMack.com

Chapter 1

Monster in My Room

If books had sound effects, right now you would hear scary, eerie music and a super-spooky howl.

That's because this adventure starts on a strangely quiet evening in October, just two weeks or so before Halloween, a holiday full of ghosts and ghouls and strange creatures from other worlds.

Twilight had turned to darkness, and outside an old house in the town of Gloucester, Massachusetts, a cold wind rubbed two tree limbs together with a high-pitched scraping sound.

Scree-eep.

Inside the house, an eleven-year-old boy lay on his bed in an upstairs bedroom lit by a single lamp, his dog curled up beside him. A laptop was on the boy's belly, and he was tapping out THE EXACT WORDS YOU ARE READING RIGHT NOW!

The boy glanced out his window, but everything was black. He looked back at his computer screen, and while one part of his mind thought about the next sentence in the book he was writing, another part wondered, *Who is the person reading this right now? Who are YOU?*

Scree-eep.

It was an eerie sound. *But only a tree branch,* he thought.

A soft ache in his belly told him dinner was already late. He glanced at the red numbers of his desk clock—7:13—and hit the Save command on his computer. His dog lifted herself and stretched. The boy set his computer down, then reached out and stroked her head.

Suddenly he became aware that something was very wrong. . . .

You probably guessed the boy was me, Ronald "Cheesie" Mack. And while I hadn't seen or heard anything, I sensed someone—or something—was nearby. Listening, waiting, watching . . .

Was it some evil demon, hideous and undead? Or perhaps a spirit reaching out to me from beyond . . .

(I have a very active imagination.)

I don't actually believe in any of that junk. Most likely it was Goon, my terrible sister (actual name = June), in the hallway just outside my bedroom, booby-trapping my door. (She once rigged a whole pile of talcum powder to drop on my head!)

I snilently (sneakily + silently) slid across my bed and gently set my stocking feet on the carpet.

Suddenly something grabbed my ankles!

Whatever held me (hands? claws?) yanked me backward. In the instant before I hit the floor I thought of how often as a small child I had lain awake wondering if a monster lurked beneath my bed. Apparently, one did!

I kicked. I twisted. I struggled. But whatever held me was very strong. It pulled harder, dragging my feet under the bed.

I screamed!

The sound that came next was a laugh . . . and then the grip on my ankles let go.

"Georgie!" I yelled.

Deeb barked. I think she was also yelling "Georgie!" but in dog language.

He belly-scooted out from under my bed, laughing so hard his face was red.

I slugged him.

"You are massively lucky kids don't get heart attacks," I scolded. "You'd be guilty of murder."

"Omigosh." Georgie chuckled. "That was so worth it."

I slugged him again. Not really hard, though. He's a total goofball, but he is still my best friend.

"How long," I asked, "were you under there?" My breathing was still ragged.

"I don't know. A long time. I came up to see if you got invited to Diana's Halloween party, but you were in the bathroom."

"So you decided to scare the crapola out of me?"

"Yep." He chuckled again and fell backward onto my bed. "So good."

"Yeah, I got invited," I said, picking up the envelope on my desk. It looked exactly like what I would've expected an invitation from Diana Mooney to look like: pink and decorated with girly wiggles and flowers and junk. "But I don't think I'm going. Are you?"

"Why not? Yeah, I am," Georgie said.

"I don't know."

"Gotta have a reason," Georgie said.

"Okay. First, I don't have a costume."

"Lame."

"Second, I'm too busy writing my next adventure."

"Liar."

"And third, it's gonna be a stupid kind of party, I bet. There'll be stupid games—"

"Stop!" Georgie held a hand up to my face. "I know the real reason. Girls," he said with a small grin.

I gave him a what-do-you-mean face.

"You, Ronald Cheese-Brain Mack, are totally, completely, and most definitely afraid of girls." Now he was grinning big-time.

"Am not," I retorted.

"Are too!" he shot back.

"Am not!"

"Are too!"

We repeated this four or five more times, louder

and louder . . . until I abruptly switched and yelled, "Are too!"

Instantly he responded, "Am not!"

And pretty soon I was yelling "Not too!" and he was screaming "Am are!" And then we both collapsed, laughing our lips off.

(You can laugh your head off. And laugh your butt off. So why can't you laugh your lips off?)

After he caught his breath, Georgie said, "Yeah, well . . . I have three words that will convince you to go to Diana's."

He took a deep breath and then just stared, waiting for me to ask.

"What?" I asked.

"Massive . . . Halloween . . . Prank."

Last year Georgie and I pulled off our first-ever Massive Halloween Prank. We recorded a radio guy giving out free tickets to a rock concert by my sister's favorite band. And when we played it back on the phone to her, she thought she had won! It was so cool we promised ourselves we'd do a Massive Halloween Prank every year for the rest of our lives.

"Oh, yeah!" I said. "Diana's party would be perfect. But who should we prank?"

"How about we come up with something that targets Eddie?" Georgie said, grinning goofily.

Eddie Chapple is sort of Georgie's main rival at school. He and Georgie are the two best players on the basketball team and also copresidents of the sixth grade. Eddie is tall and skinny, and when he moves, mostly what you notice is knees and elbows. He is kind of a tough guy but has lots of friends and would definitely be going to Diana's party. She's copresident, too. (If you read *Cheesie Mack Is Running Like Crazy!* you know why we have three presidents.)

"What kind of prank?" I asked.

Georgie jumped off my bed and pushed his grinning face right up to mine. "I dooo nooot knooow," he said. "I will start thinking about it right now!"

"You do that," I said. "And, c'mon, I am *not* afraid of girls."

"Are too," Georgie said, clamping a hand over my mouth so I couldn't contradict him.

He is much stronger than I am (he's almost twice

my size!), so at times like that I have to use strategy instead of strength.

I went totally limp.

If you do that, your opponent will almost always relax, too. And at that instant, you squirgle (This is one of my favorite made-up words: squirm + wiggle. It's in two of my other books!) out of his grasp.

It worked, and I sprang into a ferocious ninja-karate-judo pose.

Then I heard a noise downstairs.

"Lucky for you I probably have to go down for dinner now," I said in my fiercest warrior voice. "I was just getting ready to slice you into pork chops."

"You wish," he said, sliding into my desk chair. "I've already eaten. I'm going to play a game on your 'puter. Call me if you have dessert."

I screamed, "Hai-yah!" then smashed a gazillion molecules of air with a vicious karate chop, zipped into the hallway, and trotted onto the stairs.

Halfway down I stopped.

Pranking Eddie would be good, I thought. *But it'd be way better to drop our Massive Halloween Prank on one of the girls!*

Chapter 2

Giant Black Widow Spider

The downstairs noise was Granpa. He was struggling to close the back door while juggling a double armload of bags and boxes.

"Gimme some help here, kiddo," he barked, tilting his head toward the basement. "The door, please."

I pulled it open. As he clomped down the stairs, I could see what he carrying: Halloween trick-or-treat candy. Tons of it!

I like treats. Who doesn't?

This book has plenty of treats. But it has even more tricks.

If you've read any of my previous books, you already know that if someone pulls a trick on me, it's usually Goon. My sister's in eighth grade. I'm in

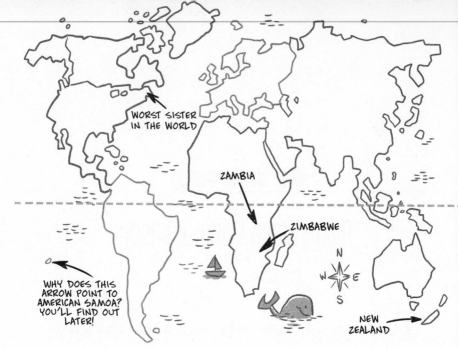

sixth. We both go to Robert Louis Stevenson Middle School, which everyone calls RLS. She is the worst sister north of the equator. (I have never been south of the equator. Maybe there's a sister in New Zealand or Zambia or Zimbabwe who's worse.)

I have a secret way to keep track of my ongoing war with Goon. It's called the Point Battle, and in *Cheesie Mack Is Not Exactly Famous*, my fourth adventure, which finished up only a week before this book starts, I got crunched by a huge Point Battle loss at the end. Even so, I was still ahead, 741–723. (In case you don't know how the Point Battle works, the rules are on my website.)

"A little help down here, Cheesie!" Granpa bellowed from the basement.

I trotted downstairs. Granpa was on his hands and knees, surrounded by about a trillion spilled hard candies.

"You can have one," Granpa said, "if you help, and if you don't tell your mother I fed you sugar right before dinner."

I kneeled and began herding the mess on the floor into one large pile. "I'll do it for two," I said, unwrapping one sour ball, plunking it into my mouth, and stashing a second in my pocket.

Most families—probably yours—hand out maybe only one measly candy bar to kids who trick-or-treat. But because Halloween is absolutely Granpa's favorite holiday, if you come to the Mack house, you get a candy bonanza!

Granpa sets up a table with a long row of decorated plastic buckets overflowing with candy. Last year there were eight of them: chocolate bars, caramels, peanut butter cups, jawbreakers, fruit leather, nut bars, gummies, and lollipops. And you get a treat from each bucket!

This makes my house just about the most popular trick-or-treat spot in Gloucester.

Granpa's been doing this since my dad was ten. Both my sister and I think it's the coolest (it's one of the few things that Goon and I agree on) . . . and so do our friends. Mom thinks it's excessive. So does my dentist.

Like squinty-evil-eyes, musical belching, and the Mack Supreme Court, giving out lots of Halloween candy is a Mack Family Tradition. If you've read my earlier books, you know about those other Mack Family Traditions. If not, you can read about them on my website . . . and while you're there, you can tell me if you have any family traditions.

When we finished scooping the spilled sweets into one of Granpa's plastic buckets, he placed it on his workbench next to the cartons of Halloween candy and said, "If you want, you can help me dump everything else into the buckets."

I started ripping open bags of every kind of great candy you can think of and emptying them into Granpa's buckets.

"And until Halloween," he said sternly, "no

mooching around down here. That goes for you and that big kid you pal around with. What's his name? Googie Stinkpot?" Granpa gave me a squinty-evil-eye, which meant he was kidding.

Of course Granpa knows Georgie Sinkoff's real name. Granpa loves to goof on me. Kidder is Granpa's middle name. (Actually he doesn't have a middle name, but if he did . . .)

Like I already said, Georgie is my best pal. Our backyards touch right where a little creek dribbles through our neighborhood. Mom says Georgie and I became friends when we were both in diapers. I can't remember that long ago, and I don't think I really want to remember what it was like to wear diapers (ugh!).

The earliest I can remember is when I was three and my family was waiting for a table in a restaurant. I grabbed on to my father's pant leg. Then the pant leg started moving, so I walked along with it. I followed it to a table and climbed into a chair. That's when I looked up and realized I had grabbed on to the leg of a STRANGER!

I don't remember anything else, but I know my mom or dad must've rescued me because, duh, if they didn't, would I be writing this now?!

What's your earliest memory? You can tell me on my website.

Here are some details about Georgie and me:

1. Georgie has braces, red-frame glasses, and radish-brown hair. (Ha! That's a typo: I meant to write "reddish," but I'm leaving it because I think his hair actually is the color of a rotted, red radish that turned brown.) He also has a very big appetite. I have brown hair, brown eyes, I like brownies . . . and I can whistle very loudly.

2. We are both in the same grade at RLS. We always had the same teacher in every grade

up to this year. Now we have only about half the same classes. But we always go to and from school and eat lunch together.

3. I am an excellent runner and second fastest on our sixth-grade cross-country team. I think Georgie is the best player on the RLS sixth-grade basketball team. Some kids think Eddie Chapple is better.

4. I have one sister whom I have already described. Georgie has one stepsister who is brand-new because his dad just got remarried. Her name is Joy. She's sixteen (I think) and a sophomore in high school. I don't know her very well, but she seems really nice.

5. Cheesiee hass bhigg ears. *[this is georrgie tryinf to ty[pe while I am si6tting on top ofd chexsie but he isd strugglin g.]*

6. Georgie and I hang out together almost all the time. When I'm writing, sometimes he butts in (like #5 above). But usually he just plops onto my bed and does one of the following (omigosh, I am doing a list inside a list!):

A) drawing or doodling. (Georgie is a really

excellent artist. He has done lots of drawings for my website.) He wants to be a cartoonist or a movie animator when he grows up. Or an airplane pilot. He loves jets.

B) homework or reading a book about airplanes or sports or some kind of mystery.

C) making fun of my ears, which stick out. I used to care, but now . . . so what? (I could erase what he puts in my books about them, but I don't, because he's my best friend, and if he wants to write something stupid, I just let him.)

7. Georgie likes Oddny Thorsdottir, a girl in our class who moved to Gloucester from Iceland over the summer. She is little bit taller than Georgie and really excellent in science and math. *[This is Georgie holding Cheesie with one arm in a no-struggle headlock this time and saying sometimes I am friends with Oddny because she helps me in those subjects because they are not my best. And anyway, Oddny's number one friend is Lana Shen, and Lana REALLY likes Cheesie, so what's*

REALLY going on, Mr. Cheese?]

My answer?

Nothing.

That's enough about the two of us.

Granpa and I were still in the basement when Mom yelled from the kitchen, "Where is everybody?"

Dad followed with, "I brought deli sandwiches, and I'm hungry!"

A few minutes later we were all at the table . . . even my sister, who had been somewhere, and I don't care where. Dad upended the bag of sandwiches in the center of the table and picked out the one for Goon. (She's a vegetarian.)

"Did you get your Halloween supplies, Pop?" Dad asked.

Granpa grunted and nodded. (I guess his mouth was full.)

Goon lifted a forkful of coleslaw and proclaimed, "All the eighth-grade cool kids are going to a Halloween party at Francine's house. Trick-or-treating is for babies."

Like I said before, I don't usually agree with my

sister because if I side with her she gets all weird and tease-ish. (Teasing is one of Goon's biggest talents.) But this time . . .

"Me too. I might not trick-or-treat this year either," I said.

"You're not going trick-or-treating?" Granpa said. "That's perfect! I've got something else for you to do." He jumped up and scurried down to the basement. We could hear him moving stuff around, ripping paper, then clomping back up the stairs. When he reappeared, he was holding something behind his back.

"This year I'm setting up my trick-or-treat table on the front lawn," he announced. "Right under the oak tree. I'll hook a rope and pulley onto one of the big branches and set up my winch motor to pull Cheesie up and down . . . wearing this!"

He pulled a totally excellent black widow spider costume from behind his back.

"You'll scare the kids!" Granpa said, grinning devilishly at me.

"Cool!" I shouted.

"This does not sound safe," Mom said.

Granpa waved a couple of spider legs at her and explained, "He'll be in a rope basket. It'll look like a spiderweb. Totally safe."

Mom looked at Granpa for a long time, then said, "Not going to happen."

Granpa harrumphed, shoved the costume onto a counter, and sat back down. He picked up his sandwich, pointed it toward Mom like he was getting ready to say something, and then just took a bite.

"Nobody should care about Halloween anyway," Goon said. "What are we celebrating? Nothing."

Granpa perked up. "You better watch how you talk about Halloween. It isn't some kind of easygoing, fun-for-all holiday like New Year's Eve or the Fourth of July. There are things about Halloween."

"What kind of things?" I asked.

Granpa's voice got all spooky. "*Strange* things."

"Give me a break," I said, flashing him a squinty-evil-eye. I expected him to give one right back to

me, but he just stared. I turned to my father.

Dad took a deep breath. "I don't know, son. Throughout history people have always wondered about things they couldn't understand or explain."

"That's right," Granpa said, waving a dill pickle in the air. "And I'm not talking about ghosts or goblins, either. That's a pile of nonsensical, fairy tale hooha. But other things . . . How about all the people who've seen UFOs?"

I frowned. "Ghosts, ghouls, *and* unidentified flying objects? They're all the same to me. Total baloney," I said, suddenly realizing there was baloney in my sandwich.

Granpa took a chomp on his pickle, then pointed the stump at me. "Think about it. If a space alien wanted to fly down here and visit us helpless earthlings, what better time to do it than Halloween?"

I looked from Granpa to Dad. No squinty-evil-eyes from either one. In fact, they were both staring in a way that made me weirdly uncomfortable.

I was really sure Granpa was pulling my leg . . . so why did a shiver go up my spine?

Chapter 3

Life on Other Planets

The next morning the weather was good, so Georgie and I rode our bikes to school. We sat through CORE, which is two periods in a row of social studies and language arts, then, like every day, we split up. He went to math, and I went to science.

Getting into my science room wasn't easy, though.

Kandy DeLeon, who is sixth-grade vice president, and Livia Grant, our treasurer, were in the hallway in front of the door to room 220 with four other girls. All were in their cheerleader outfits. To them, I guess, the last few minutes before third period started was the perfect time to practice because they were flinging their arms around and doing some dance moves while whispering loudly, "R-L-S. We're the best!"

(You are not allowed to yell in our school hallways.)

At first I couldn't get into the room because of all the gwirling (girl + whirling) arms, but finally I just squedged (squeeze + edged) my way through.

Kandy bonked me on the head.

Not hard, but I think on purpose.

"Good morning," Mr. Amato said as soon as the bell sounded. He is almost always cheery. He is also short, bald, and plumpishly round. His head looks like a small beach ball on top of a huge beach ball . . . if beach balls had arms and legs. His class is super interesting because he is full of surprises. Last week he showed us hard-to-believe optical illusions. I put a few on my website.

Mr. Amato picked up his textbook and announced, "Today we start a new topic. Please open to chapter twelve."

Everyone started flipping pages. Lana got there first. " 'Astronomy: The Solar System and Beyond,' " she read just loud enough for me to hear.

Mr. Amato rubbed his bald head. "I apologize for being absent yesterday. I had a little crisis at home. Lost pet. How was my substitute?"

Kandy's hand shot up. Mr. Amato pointed to her.

"Bogus. Supremely bogus," Kandy said. "He told lame jokes and boring stories. Luckily for us, he finally told us to take out a book and read."

Because we had just finished chapter six ("Our Five Senses") in our science textbook, I read the next chapter ("Understanding the Earth"). It was all about earthquakes, lava, minerals, and an amazing volcano called Mount Tambora, which is in Indonesia, a country between Asia and Australia.

In 1815, Mount Tambora blew its top. It went from being 14,100 feet high to 9,354 feet high. That's almost a mile of volcano gone kablooey!

Scientists say it was the largest volcanic eruption in human history. It was so loud, people more than 1,200 miles away heard the explosion! It produced a

BEFORE   AFTER

huge amount of smoke and ash that floated around the world and blocked out lots of sunlight. In Europe, the following year was called the "Year Without a Summer" because it got so cold. In the United States, it snowed in June! Crops failed all over the northern hemisphere, causing the worst famine of the nineteenth century.

"I'm sorry the substitute was not up to your standards," Mr. Amato said with a smile and a slight bow. "I shall attempt to have perfect attendance for the remainder of the year."

He clicked around on his computer until an image of the nighttime sky came up on our class's computer screen.

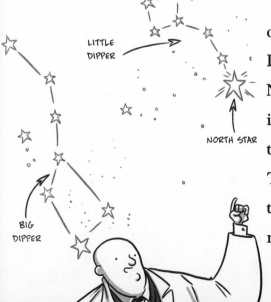

LITTLE DIPPER

NORTH STAR

BIG DIPPER

Mr. Amato pointed out the Big Dipper, the Little Dipper, and the North Star. "Stargazing was very important to ancient civilizations. They used the stars and the movement of the moon and the planets to know when to plant crops and how to find their way from place to place. Question: How did the ancient peoples observe these heavenly objects?"

Glenn raised his hand. "With the naked eye. Telescopes weren't invented until the seventeenth century. Microscopes, too."

"Exactly right, Glenn. The optical devices you mentioned became important tools in many areas of science." Mr. Amato pointed at some writing in a corner of the whiteboard. "With that in mind, your next assignment is a report or a hands-on project about telescopes, microscopes, or anything that has a lens . . . anything that deals with optics."

You've probably seen the *opt-* prefix before. It means the word has something to do with eyes or vision, like *optometrist* (vision doctor), *optician* (someone who makes eyeglasses), and *optopus* (a sea creature I just made up with an eyeball on each of its tentacles . . . hee-hee).

Georgie has a microscope at home, but we'd already used it for our last science project (tiny, disgusting critters on his eyelashes . . . They were in my third adventure, *Cheesie Mack Is Running Like*

Crazy!). So I decided, right then and there, to make a periscope. A periscope (*peri-* means "around," and *scopus* means "to look") is a device that uses mirrors to let you look around corners or anything else. Submarines have periscopes that let the crew see what's on the surface, even when it's underwater.

Mr. Amato continued, "This coming weekend, something quite special will happen in the sky, something you all can see for yourselves if the weather is clear. The Orionid meteor shower."

He clicked something on his computer, and the image on our screen changed to the whitish arc of a

shooting star (which, you probably know, is a meteor, *not* a star).

"How many of you have ever seen a meteor
shower?"

Most of the class raised hands. I did. Lana did not.

Mr. Amato continued talking about meteors and
optics and astronomy for over half the period, and it
was pretty interesting, but then Glenn posed a question that changed the subject, and things got even
more interesting.

"From the time the Earth formed," Glenn asked,
"how long did it take for the first life to evolve?"

"About a billion years," Mr. Amato answered, "but
that's somewhat misleading because for most of that
time, the Earth was too hot for anything, and the atmosphere was poisonous."

"But it could've happened a lot faster on other
planets, right?" Eddie suggested.

"Perhaps," Mr. Amato said. "It's an interesting
speculation."

Lots of hands went up after that. Because of all the
sci-fi movies kids watch, almost every question was
about extraterrestrials or UFOs.

Weird coincidence, I thought. *Granpa was talking about UFOs last night.*

I raised my hand and asked, "Why is it 'extra'? And what's a 'terrestrial'?"

"*Extra* means 'beyond,' and *terrestrial* comes from *terra*, which means 'earth.' Extraterrestrials are life-forms that come from beyond the earth," Mr. Amato explained.

Kandy whispered loudly to Lana, "Tentacle Monsters from Mars." They both giggled.

Mr. Amato must've also talked about ETs and UFOs in his fourth-period science class (Georgie and Oddny are in that one), because at lunch, Oddny said, "It just doesn't make sense that Earth is the only planet in this gigantic universe with intelligent life."

I hadn't really thought much about it. Since Glenn Philips is the smartest kid in sixth grade, I decided to ask him. "What's your opinion, Glenn?"

Glenn put down his sandwich and cleared his throat. "Well, I am not an expert on extraterrestrial life."

"ETs," Georgie mumbled through his mouthful of potato chips.

"But there are scientists who would agree with Oddny," Glenn continued.

Oddny smiled.

There were eight kids at our table. Everyone was listening to Glenn. "They say that there are billions and billions of stars and lots of them have planets circling them. But take Neptune or Mercury in our solar system. Planets like those would not be suitable for life."

"You'd burn up on Mercury," Lana said. "Too close to the sun."

"And freeze your butt solid on Neptune," Eddie said.

Glenn nodded. "So astronomers are looking for what they call a Goldilocks planet."

"One with bears," Georgie said.

"And a little lost girl!" I added.

Everybody laughed, and Georgie and I high-fived. His finger was almost healed from his basketball injury, so his splint would be coming off soon. (I described how his broken finger didn't stop him from playing basketball in my fourth adventure, *Cheesie Mack Is Not Exactly Famous*.)

"Not exactly," Glenn said. "In the fairy tale, Goldilocks tries the porridge. Remember?"

Suddenly I knew just what Glenn was leading up to.

"The first bowl she tried was too hot," he said. "The second one was too cold."

"And the third one was just right!" Lana blurted excitedly.

"So if we find a not-too-hot, not-too-cold planet that's 'just right,'" Oddny said, "then it'll have life on it."

"Not necessarily," Glenn said. "Not every Goldilocks planet will have life on it. And if it does have life, what if it's not intelligent life?"

"Like some of the kids at this school," Eddie stuck in.

"Like Cheesie!" Georgie shouted.

"Like Georgie!" I yelled at the exact same time.

Then we both laughed, which got everyone else laughing.

"I absolutely believe that we are not alone," Oddny said after the table quieted down.

"But you can't just believe," I said. "That's like believing in zombies or vampires."

"I might actually be a vampire," Kandy said. "I have pointy, sharp teeth." She leaned over and pretended to bite Lana's neck.

Lana ignored her. "But what about all the people who swear they've seen UFOs?"

"The great majority of those sightings turn out to be weather balloons or airplanes, or something else man-made," Glenn said. "They might look suspicious at first, but they turn out to be totally explainable."

"But not *all* of them," Oddny responded.

"Okay, sure," I responded, thinking about what Granpa had said last night. "Maybe some of them are unexplained; that doesn't mean they're real. You need evidence. You need something like a message from a UFO." I sort of stood up, cupped my hands around my mouth, and spoke in a high-pitched, wiggly voice, "Greetings, earthlings! What's going on?"

Most of the kids thought it was funny. Oddny did not.

Glenn nodded and then shook his head. "I don't

think there's any record of a message from a UFO, but there are scientists who search for signals from outer space."

"I've got a question," Georgie said. "Even if we did get signals from a UFO or from outer space, how would we understand them? The real world isn't like in sci-fi movies, where every weird creature speaks English."

Glenn nodded. "You're right. You'd need something everyone would understand, like math. One plus one is two no matter what planet you're on. I suspect the first message Earth will ever get from an alien civilization—if we ever do get one—will be communicated using math."

Everyone got kind of quiet. I was thinking about ETs, and I bet everyone else was, too.

The end-of-lunch bell rang. We picked up our trays and split up to go to our lockers. As Georgie and I were getting our books (our lockers are next to each other), he suddenly grabbed my arm, then leaned back against the wall of lockers and started tapping one finger against his chin.

"What?" I asked.

"I have the totally greatest Great Idea I have ever had."

"Uh-oh," I said. "Here comes trouble."

Georgie is a very creative guy. He comes up with lots of ideas, some of which are Great. But I have to be careful, because some of them are Not-So-Great. (Like the Mouse Plot in my first book, *Cheesie Mack Is Not a Genius or Anything*. If you read it, you know how that turned out!)

I put my backpack on. "What's your Great Idea?"

"I absolutely know what to do for our Massive Halloween Prank," he said with a big grin. "Oddny thinks there are ET alien space creatures out there right now just waiting to send messages to us here on Earth, right?"

I nodded and looked at the clock on the corridor wall. Three minutes until the tardy bell.

"So, we send her an actual message from space!" He slammed his locker shut to emphasize how Great his Great Idea was.

"An *actual* message from space?" I asked.

Georgie gave me an are-you-stupid look. "Not an *actual* message. Just something that *seems* like one."

The last few kids in the hall were scurrying away. "But how can we do that?" I asked. "I mean, how do you fake a message from space?"

"I came up with the Great Idea," Georgie said, lifting his backpack onto his shoulders. "You figure out the details."

It was a Great Idea. I pounded on his backpack and grinned. "I'll do it!"

Even though the corridor was deserted, Georgie pulled me close and whispered in my ear, "The name of our secret operation will be 'Plan It.' Get it? Planet."

"Got it!" I said, looking up at the clock again. One minute.

When I looked down, Georgie had taken off for his class. I sprinted to mine, even though running in the hallways is totally against school rules.

I was tardy to Spanish class, but I didn't care. All I had to do now was figure just one thing out and we'd have the best Hallow in the history of Eens!

Chapter 4

Up Periscope! Banzai!

On most days, Georgie and I stay after school because I go to cross-country practice and Georgie has a basketball workout in the gym.

"Have you figured it out yet?" Georgie asked me while we were changing clothes in the locker room.

"Give me 'til the end of practice," I replied. I bet I sounded more confident than I felt. I'd been thinking about the Massive Halloween Prank nonstop since lunch and hadn't come up with a single idea.

The boys' and girls' sixth-grade XC teams (that's the abbreviation for cross-country) work out together. At the end of our runs, Coach Tunavelov (we call him Coach T) sits us all down on the grass and goes over our progress charts.

"Good job," Coach T said to Lana and Josh. "Slow, steady improvement. That's what I like to see."

(I think that's what he said. My mind was in outer space . . . if you know what I mean.)

"Chapple," Coach T called out to Eddie. "Your last race? Nine seconds better on the final mile than your previous run. Excellent."

"Mack," Coach T continued, walking up to where I squatted on the grass.

I'd been staring at the sky. Suddenly I was paying attention.

"You are consistently in the top finishers," he said. "But I think you can do better. Your closing kick is good, but I want to see you set a little faster pace at the beginning."

I nodded. He was right. I tended to start slowly to conserve my energy. Maybe I could change my strategy.

Coach T went through the rest of the team and ended with, "Philips."

Glenn, who was flat on his back, popped up. He had run really fast at practice and was still panting.

"Most improved on the whole squad. You've cut almost twenty seconds off your time. Great job! Good work, all of you. That's it."

We stood and started in. Eddie came up next to me and plopped his elbow onto my shoulder. As we walked, he leaned his pointy nose and pointy chin and pointy eyebrows in close and said quietly, "I'm excellent. You're consistent. Hmm. Which do I think is better?" Then he trotted ahead of me into the gym.

Eddie is very competitive. He and I almost always have the best times on our team. And even though he beats me more than I beat him, he still has to say something to prove it.

After changing back into my regular clothes, I met up with Georgie at the bike racks.

"Have you figured out how we're going to trick Oddny and Lana?" he asked, then popped a terrible wheelie and headed out of the school parking lot. (He is not particularly excellent with bike tricks.)

"I'll think of something," I yelled after him. A couple of blocks later I called out, "Hey, do you want to work with me on Amato's science project?"

"It's . . . not . . . due . . . for . . . a . . . week," Georgie puffed.

We were powering up a hill, so both of us were out of breath.

"True. . . . How . . . about . . . we . . . build . . . periscopes? . . . It'll . . . be . . . fun," I huffed back.

It was just a simple suggestion. Little did I know that optics was going to be a part of our Massive Halloween Prank!

When we went over the crest of the hill, Georgie started pumping hard. I coasted down. By the time he reached the bottom, he was way ahead of me.

I caught up at a red light.

"A periscope would be good," Georgie said as we pedaled past Rocky Neck Elementary (our old school) and turned onto Eureka Avenue.

"Hello, Ms. Prott!" I shouted.

"Hello, Ms. Prott!" Georgie echoed.

We weren't yelling to anyone we saw. We were just riding by The Haunted Toad (it's a spooky old house mentioned a lot in my first book). We do that every time we pass by, even though Ms. Prott is never out front or in the window or probably can't even hear us. (She is almost a hundred years old!) But because she's been so nice to us, we always yell hello to her even if she doesn't know.

A few minutes later we laid our bikes against my garage and walked into my backyard. Granpa was raking leaves into mounds.

"Don't go bouncing around and messing up my piles!" he shouted. There were four big humps, each in a different part of the yard . . . and he was heaping up a fifth.

I wasn't planning to jump in the leaves, but I guess Granpa was remembering me when I was younger, when there would've been no way I could've resisted leaping around in one or two of those piles.

Here's something I have noticed about parents and grandparents. It always seems that they think of us kids the way we used to be, not the way we are now. I guess it's because we're always growing, and they're not always used to the new us.

"Granpa? Do you have any mirrors?" I asked. He has a workshop in our basement. It's packed with all kinds of junk.

"What size? And what do you need them for?"

"Georgie and I want to make a periscope. It's for science class."

"Okay. I tell you what." He dropped the rake and began walking toward the house. "You boys finish raking and then scoop all these leaves into those bags over there, and I'll set up everything you need on my workbench."

I yelled after him, "Actually we need two periscopes! One for each of us!"

He made a thumbs-up sign and went into the house.

While he was gone, we raked and bagged all the leaves, but I have to admit there was a spectacular amount of leaping, jumping, and somersault pile-flopping.

[Georgie here: I deserved a perfect ten on my Double Monkey Butt Spinner, but the judge was busy doing a much worse trick in another pile of leaves.]

Not true. My Triple Screaming Headfirst Pancake was most awesome, but no one was watching.

Eventually we finished and went down to the basement, where Granpa had cleared a workspace for us and set out all the materials we might need. He was lying back in his recliner chair, eyes closed. It might seem weird to have an easy chair in a basement workshop, but Granpa says, "Most people sleep at night and stay up in the day because that's what they've been told to do. Not me. I sleep when I'm tired and don't when I'm not." And in our home, the basement is sort of Granpa's private space.

On his workbench were two long cardboard tubes, glue, four small mirrors, some heavy paper, a dead chipmunk, and a pair of scissors. (I'm kidding about the chipmunk . . . and why do we call it a *pair* of scissors? If you only had one side, would it be a scissor?)

It took us about an hour, and our fingers got sticky from the glue, but here's what we made. The plans for making a periscope are on my website, if you want to build one for yourself.

MIRROR

MIRROR

Georgie and I went outside to test our creations. But a spy needs an enemy to spy on.

My sister!

She was sitting at our backyard picnic table with Drew, having a "private" conversation. She was snuggled right next to him and sort of leaning on his shoulder.

One periscope-toting spy might have stayed secret. But two not-so-quiet spies with secret spying devices peeking around the corner of the house were just too obvious. Goon spotted us, yanked her head off Sweetie-Pie Drew's shoulder (barf!), and got instantly embarrassed. It was a two-point victory for me, increasing my Point Battle lead to 743–723.

In my many years of arguing and fighting with Goon, I have learned one useful fact. It takes almost nothing to get her angry. She jumped up and came after us. Well, actually she came after me. Goon never messes with Georgie. Two reasons:

1. He's not her brother.
2. He's bigger than she is.

There's no way Goon can ever catch me. I am way faster than her. I zipped around the side of the house.

You probably remember that Goon is a really excellent dancer who practices ballet all the time, so she is very agile. But I am also very agile . . . and even more important, I am very tricky.

So here's what I did.

When we got to the front yard, I was so far ahead of her that she sort of gave up and stopped running. Everyone knows there's no fun in being chased by your sister if she gives up, so I suddenly stopped running, spun a U-turn, and ran directly at her, screaming, "Banzai!" and waving my periscope in the air like a sword.

Completely confused by my charge, she stepped backward, tripped over her own feet, and fell on her butt.

Victory!

I laughed, yelled "Banzai!" again, and gave myself one more point: 744–723!

(Lots of people think *banzai* is a Japanese word that means "Charge!" But I just looked it up. It actually means "ten thousand years" and originally was used to wish long life to someone. So maybe I was being an excellent brother.)

Goon did not think I was particularly excellent. She jumped up, angrier than ever, screaming, "You bad, bad boy! I'm going to punish you severely!"

(That is definitely NOT what she said, but the people who publish this book definitely won't print her actual words.)

Off I went again! I zoomed around to the back-yard, all the time sort of laughing to myself. Suddenly Drew jumped out from I-don't-know-where and tried to grab me. I dodged him easily (he is a slow lump), but I dropped my periscope.

Before I could double back and retrieve it, Goon pounced, bounced, trounced, and flounced!

(Cats *pounce*. Balls *bounce*. Everyone knows those words. *Trounce* means to beat badly. And when you *flounce*, you throw your body around like an exaggerating maniac . . . which describes Goon perfectly!)

When she had finished with what I'm sure she thought was a victory dance, Goon stood on top of the flattened, massacred, and destroyed remains of my science project, grinning.

(She got one point because smashing my periscope was sort of an insult, and since Drew was watching, I

had to double it to two. Now it was 744–725.)

She thought she had beaten me, but I had one more trick up my sleeve. I slipped my cell phone out of my pocket and snapped a picture of her standing over my crushed periscope.

"Evidence!" I shouted, and sprinted into the house. Georgie was right behind me. My dog, Deeb (in case you forgot her name), who had been lying in the hallway, yipped once and zoomed up the stairs after us. I could hear Goon yelling long after we were in my room with the door locked.

Georgie and I were so excited, we couldn't stop jumping around the room. Finally I dropped into my desk chair, and Georgie flopped onto my bed.

"That was awesome!" he said, peering at me through his periscope. "Are you really going to show that photo to your parents?"

I shook my head. I rarely tattle on Goon. (But sometimes I do. I'm not perfect.)

"Nah. I took the picture for Mr. Amato. We'll both use your periscope, but I'll show him this photo to prove I actually made my own."

(And bonus! I emailed the picture to Goon, which caused her to scream so loudly, Mom took away her cell phone until after breakfast. No texting all evening! That punishment was worth four more points to me. Now it was 748–725.)

I went to bed that night thinking hard about how to create a message from outer space. There were only a few days until Diana's party. If we were going to do a really excellent prank on Lana and Oddny, I needed an idea.

Sometimes I dream up my best ideas when I'm sleeping.

Chapter 5

Brain Freeze

Not this time.

In the morning I was no closer to solving my Massive Halloween Prank problem.

As I was finishing breakfast, Dad asked, "I understand your periscope got broken."

Goon pretended to pay no attention, but I saw her give me a glary face.

"How did you know?" I asked.

"I know lots of things around here," Dad replied. "Anyway, about your science project . . . how would you like to do something with my telescope instead?"

I was surprised. "I didn't know you had one."

"It's in the attic. I bet I haven't touched it in fifteen years. Birthday present from Pop."

Granpa nodded. "It's a good one."

Georgie appeared at my back door. "C'mon, Cheesie! We're gonna be late."

"Nah. I don't need it for the homework. Georgie and I made two periscopes. We still have one left. We'll be okay." I ran out and hopped on my bike. Georgie was circling in the street, waiting for me.

I had barely gone ten feet when it hit me. "Georgie!"

He changed course and pedaled over. "What?"

"Plan It needs a message from aliens, right? Well, how do you see a message from outer space? With a telescope, right?"

"Yeah . . . so?" he said.

"We can use my dad's telescope!" I said triumphantly. "He's got a good one. I didn't even know about it until just now."

Georgie returned to pedaling in circles. "How do we get the girls to look through your telescope?"

"I haven't figured that out yet," I said. "Race you to school!"

I am an excellent bike rider. As usual, I beat him . . . even though the whole way I was thinking,

Telescopes. Messages. Aliens. Outer space. Girls.
Finally I thought, *This is impossible.*

Granpa says impossible problems get solved one of three ways.

1. Hard work. "You lay your shoulder into the problem and push . . . and you never let up!"

2. A new approach. "Look at the problem from another angle. Use different tools. Put some oil on it or hit it with a brick!"

3. A stroke of good fortune. "Sometimes you've got no other choice than to wait for Lady Luck to drop a gold nugget in your lap."

It took all day, but after school we got a #3 nugget.

Neither Georgie nor I had sports practice (there was some kind of teacher meeting), so we were getting on our bikes to go home when Oddny and Lana walked by.

"You know what Lana and I are doing on Sunday?" Oddny said. "We're watching the Orionids."

"Is that a hockey team?" Georgie asked.

"It's the meteor shower Mr. Amato mentioned in class yesterday."

Lana said, "Mr. Amato told us it was okay for our

optics project if we took some pictures of them shooting across the sky."

Georgie looked at me and opened his eyes real wide. "That's such a cool idea," he said, turning back to the girls. "Cheese and I made periscopes."

"Only one survived," I muttered.

"That's cool, too," Lana agreed. "Hey, Oddny and I are going to my house right now to have ice cream. You want some?"

Georgie shouted, "Yes!" before I could say a word.

"Hold on a minute," I said. "I forgot something in my locker." I motioned for Georgie. "Come with me."

I started trotting back into school. Georgie shrugged, got off his bicycle, and followed me.

Here was my problem. I was already getting teased at school by Josh and Eddie and lots of the girls for talking to Lana a lot. Kids were asking, Did I like her? Was she my girlfriend? Would I be hanging out with her at Diana's party?

Kandy actually passed me a totally embarrassing note at lunch last week.

Come on! I have said it before. Lana is not my girlfriend. I don't have a girlfriend. End of story.

Georgie is more interested in girls than I am. So I wonder if someday soon he is going to go weird on me and decide he wants to spend more time with Oddny than with me.

[Georgie here: No way! End of story.]

"I don't want to go with the girls," I told Georgie once we were out of sight inside the school.

"Yes, you do," he countered. "They just told us how we're going to make Plan It work."

"Huh?"

"They're going to watch some O'Reilly meteors this weekend."

"Orionids," I said.

"Whatever." Georgie grabbed me by the shoulders. "Don't you get it? They're going to be looking into space. There's no better time to send them a message from little green men. Let's hang out with them now. Once we're at Lana's house, you'll ask if we can watch with them."

"Why me?"

"Because you're so scared of girls, no one will suspect you're up to something."

I hated to say it, but it was another of Georgie's Great Ideas. And Granpa had been right. Lady Luck had just given us a gold Orionid nugget.

Just then Kandy, Livia, and a couple of other girls walked by.

"Okay, but you go ahead without me," I whispered. "I don't want anyone to see me leaving with Lana and Oddny. I'll meet you there."

"You're weird. But okay. No problem," Georgie said. Then he grinned. "I'll tell the girls your underwear was on backward and you had to go to the bathroom to change."

Georgie ran back out to where the girls were waiting, picked up his bike, and started walking away from school with them. I waited until they were out of sight around the corner, then walked back out to the bike rack.

"You better hurry if you want to catch up to your girlfriend," Kandy said loudly enough for every nearby kid to overhear.

"Ha, ha. I'm going home," I replied, and rode off.

I had to pedal six blocks in the wrong direction before I could double back and head toward Lana's house. Georgie and the girls were just starting up the last hill when I caught up with them. A few minutes later we were sitting at Lana's kitchen table while Mrs. Shen (she's really nice) served us. At first we ate ice cream mostly silently; then we ate more ice cream and talked about meteors.

"What are they made of?" Georgie picked up a huge, drippy glob and devoured it. He was yumming 'scream. (I made that up in my last book! It's what you say when you're eating ice cream and loving it!)

"They're rocks, I think," Lana said.

"Are there just giant bunches of random rocks floating around in space?" Georgie asked. "Where do they come from?"

"I know," Oddny said brightly. "They come from—" Suddenly she stopped, pinched her eyes half shut, and moaned, "Brain freeze."

I bet every kid has had a brain freeze. You eat or drink something cold really fast and all of a sudden

you get a sharp pain like a headache.

(I'm going to stop writing for a moment and find out what causes brain freeze.)

* * * * *

I asked Granpa. He said the pain comes from chunks of ice forming inside brain cells, and that every time it happens, brain cells die . . . and you get stupider. But then he gave me a squinty-evil-eye, so I knew he was kidding.

Then I asked my mother. She didn't know. But she was really curious. She loves ice cream. "It happens to me all the time," she admitted.

So we looked it up together online. We discovered that it's also called an "ice cream headache." (That makes sense!) It happens because the roof of your mouth gets really cold, which somehow causes nerves to send a signal to the brain that gets interpreted as a headache. If you get a brain freeze, the best way to stop it is to warm the roof of your mouth. One way is to press your tongue against it.

(That's enough brain freeze research. Now back to Lana's house, where Oddny's brain freeze was causing her to squirm in her chair.)

* * * * *

Mrs. Shen handed Oddny a glass of warm water. I guess it worked, because a couple of swallows later, Oddny said, "Whew," and finished the thought that had been interrupted by her brain freeze. "You must've been asleep in class, Georgie. Mr. Amato told us the Orionids are leftover scraps from Halley's Comet, which is very famous, and once a year the earth goes through a bunch of them."

"I was right!" Georgie grinned. "It is bunches of random rocks floating around in space. How big are they?"

"Most of them are tiny. Like grains of sand," Oddny explained. "But they still light up the sky."

I was only halfway listening. It was time to begin setting the trap.

"Um . . . could we maybe . . ." I hemmed and hawed because I didn't want to sound too eager. "Um . . . maybe Georgie and I could come over and watch the Orionids with you guys on Sunday?"

"Sure!" Lana said quickly.

"It's a very good idea for you boys," Mrs. Shen said. "I will make a homemade Chinese meal before you watch the sky. Do you like Chinese food?"

"A lot!" Georgie quickly replied.

"Very good," Mrs. Shen said. "Do you know how to eat with chopsticks?"

Georgie shook his head and moaned, "I'll starve to death."

"I will teach you," Mrs. Shen said with a big smile.

"Cheesie'll bring his father's telescope to take pictures of the meteors," Georgie offered.

Lana then said something to me, but I didn't hear her because I was thinking hard about our Massive Halloween Prank: *We'll do it here on Sunday with the telescope. Now all we need is the message from outer space. . . .*

Lana tapped me on the arm to get my attention. "Bringing your telescope will really help us. Thanks."

I didn't say anything back. All I could think about was that when Kandy and the other girls heard about our meteor watching, I'd be teased at school for sure. So I gobbled up a big spoonful of ice cream and pretended to have brain freeze.

I don't know why.

I just did.

Chapter BBB

Antarctic Expedition

"What else can go wrong?" Mackron hissed through clenched teeth. He had vowed to be the first man to make it to the South Pole single-handedly. He was unafraid of ice, rock, wind, and intense cold, but the weather had turned on him. Blizzard after blizzard after blizzard . . .

For three weeks the weather had forced Mackron, the world-famous explorer, to remain in the cramped astronomical research station, eighty-five miles from his goal, with only Professor Oddlan for company.

And what an odd companion Oddlan was.

The strange scientist studied comets. She loved comets. She talked about nothing but comets . . . except when she spoke about meteors.

Oddlan had not left the research station for three years. She lived and worked through six months of constant daylight followed by six months of constant darkness. And all of it alone. She had repeated this insane cycle three times. She had to be completely crazy.

But the worst thing was the food. Oddlan had used up most of her supplies, and now all that was left was a huge supply of ice cream . . . all of it licorice-flavored.

Mackron dropped his head into his hands and mumbled almost silently, "Disaster . . ."

* * * * *

I really like reading books about exploration, so just now I decided to write one of my mini-chapters about a courageous explorer.

Of course his name is Mackron. You can probably guess why.

Professor Oddlan is a combination of Oddny and Lana.

And if you can't figure out why the only food is ice cream, you must have completely forgotten what you read in the last chapter.

I picked licorice ice cream because this month the ice cream shop in Gloucester is selling two special flavors in honor of Halloween: pumpkin and licorice. As you know, I am a kid who likes adventures, so when Granpa took me there, I ordered a scoop of each. My cone was bright orange and pure black. It looked terrific.

(What is your favorite ice cream flavor? I'm doing a poll on my website.)

The pumpkin ice cream was okay, but even though I like black licorice, it does not make a delicious ice cream.

And it turned my tongue black!

But it wasn't all bad. When I got home, I tricked Mom, "I feel kind of sick. And my throat hurts."

"Open your mouth and stick out your tongue," she said.

I did.

My mother shrieked!

Chapter 6

More Brainpower

Lana's house sits higher up on a hill in Gloucester than ours do, so Georgie and I were able to coast almost all the way home. He rode ahead of me the whole time, so I was alone with my thoughts.

You guessed it. . . . They were all about Plan It.

We parked our bikes in my garage. Deeb was there to greet us. There was still about an hour before dinner, and I was tired of thinking, so I grabbed an old tennis ball off a shelf.

"You want to?" I asked Georgie, holding the ball up for him to see.

I didn't have to explain.

"Sure," he replied, jogging just ahead of me into my backyard. My pooch immediately spotted the ball in my hand and was ready for our game of Deeb-away.

Deeb-away is almost like keep-away, except in Deeb-away my dog is always the one in the middle. Here the way the game works:

1. Georgie and I stand about twenty feet apart.

2. We throw the ball to each other, and Deeb tries to get it.

3. Every throw has to bounce at least once.

4. If the throw is bad, causing the catcher to miss it, the catcher gets a point.

5. If the catcher drops a good throw, the thrower gets a point.

6. If Deeb gets the ball before the catcher touches it, then it's a bad throw, and the catcher gets two points.

7. If the ball hits Deeb, the catcher gets three points.

Georgie and I are almost evenly matched when we play Deeb-away because he is a better thrower, but I am quicker on my feet. We are both excellent catchers.

Best of all, Deeb loves the game.

The score was 14–12 (I was losing). I raised my arm to throw. Deeb eyed me, ready for whatever. Then I dropped my arm. I had come to an unfortunate decision. "We can't do Plan It."

Deeb started jumping around and whining. She didn't want the game to stop.

"Why not?" Georgie asked.

I'd been working my brain until it hurt. And like

the title of my first book says, I'm not a genius or anything. "I have no idea how to fool the girls into thinking they're getting a message from outer space."

I threw the tennis ball to Georgie, but Deeb grabbed it. I wasn't keeping score anymore.

Georgie stared up at the twilight sky. "Don't give up. We'll think of something."

I wasn't so sure.

At dinner that evening I asked my father if we could borrow his telescope. Even if Plan It was dead, Georgie and I had promised to let the girls use it, and we could still look at meteors and planets and stuff.

When it got dark my father and I set it up outside, and he showed me how to use it. Georgie wasn't there. His dad and stepmom had taken him to a basketball game at the high school. Joy, his new stepsister, is one of the star players.

The next day at school, nothing interesting happened.

It's weird how you can be full of energy and all excited about something (Plan It), and that makes everything fun and interesting. But then, if your big exciting thing sort of dies, everything gets dull and boring. That's what school was like . . . until the very end of the day.

We had done a shorter-than-usual XC team run because it was Friday. The weather was nice, and there were flocks of birds overhead, migrating south for the winter. It should've been a fun run except, like I said, everything seemed dull and boring. Even worse, I was still going to Lana's house on Sunday even though now the only reason was because Georgie had promised them I would bring my dad's telescope.

Georgie was already in the locker room changing out of his basketball clothes when I came in with Glenn and the rest of the guys on the XC team.

"Hey, Glenn," I said, untying my shoes. "I've got a question. We need to photograph some shooting stars on Sunday night, so Georgie and I . . ."

He looked interested.

". . . are going to set up my dad's telescope at Lana's house—"

"A telescope is a bad choice," Glenn said.

"What?" I said.

"Meteors shoot across the sky rapidly," Glenn explained. "A telescope magnifies only a very small part of the sky. How will you know where to aim it? You'll miss every one."

"It's better just to use your eyes?" I asked.

Glenn nodded.

Glenn was so smart. Was there any problem he couldn't solve . . . ?

Suddenly I knew there was a chance to save Plan It!

"Glenn, can you keep a secret?" I whispered.

Now he was very interested. He nodded again. Georgie looked at me curiously.

"Okay. Here's the deal. Georgie and I want to play a prank on Oddny and Lana."

Georgie's eyes widened. He stood behind Glenn, silently and frantically waving his hands no-no-stop.

I ignored Georgie. I knew what I was doing. "We want the girls to look through the telescope and see a fake signal from Martians or some other spacemen," I continued.

Glenn grinned. "You guys are bad."

"The problem is, this is a super-complex prank, and we can't figure out how to do it. We need your brainpower. Help us. It'll be fun."

Georgie's hand waving switched from no-no-stop to yes-yes-keep-going.

Glenn hadn't given me an answer yet, so I added, "Every year Georgie and I do a Massive Halloween Prank. This year—well, this is only our second year—we need you to be part of our team."

Glenn sat on the bench in front of his locker just staring at nothing for a long time. He was thinking (which is exactly what he's best at). Finally he spoke. "Okay. I'll do it."

Georgie grabbed Glenn in a bear hug and lifted him in the air. I never saw Glenn grin like that!

After we left school, I explained the whole situation while we pushed our bikes alongside him (he's a walker). It was a short walk, only four blocks. But when we got to his house, he said, "I've got it. I know what to do. What's Lana's address?"

I told him, and we spent a few minutes looking at a map of Gloucester on Glenn's computer. Then we went into his backyard.

"Lana lives up there," he said, pointing to a nearby hill. "Her house is the green one with the red chimney. If we can see it from here, then you'll be able to see my house from there. So, if we raise the signal generator high enough above my backyard, then aim your telescope from her house . . ."

He looked straight up, then back at the red chimney far up on the hill.

"Yes. That should work." Glenn looked pleased. "Let's go back inside, and I'll print out a list of materials you'll need to get."

I had no idea what Glenn was planning to do. I mean, what the heck is a signal generator? But he is the smartest sixth grader at RLS, so I wasn't worried.

Chapter 7

Balloon Buoy Boys

When we got back to my house, my mom was still at work (she's an air-traffic controller at Logan Airport), and Granpa was out driving one of the limos somewhere. By the time Dad finished making dinner, it was too late to get any of the stuff on Glenn's list, so Georgie and I decided we'd get an early start the next morning (Saturday). It wasn't a school night, so Georgie slept over.

Beep.

In the morning that's what woke me. I must've been dreaming about Glenn's list, because the first thing I did (I was half-asleep) was to grab it off my night table.

Materials Needed:

Brightly colored heavy-duty balloons (3 big or 6 medium)

Black heavy-duty balloons (6 big or 12 medium)

1 small tank of helium gas

50 yards good-quality kite string

100 yards lightweight, thin-gauge, black insulated two-strand wire

1 high-intensity LED

1 lantern battery

Beep.

"What's that noise?" Georgie asked from under the pillow that covered his head.

"One of our smoke detectors must have a low battery, I guess." I examined Glenn's list. "I don't even know what some of these things are, so how can we possibly get them? Something called a lantern battery, a whole bunch of special wire, balloons . . . and what is LED?"

"I think it's what's in the center of a pencil," Georgie said, yawning.

"Or what's in the center of your skull," I joked. I opened my bedroom door to go to the bathroom, but Goon was just going in. I sat at my desk.

Georgie climbed out of bed and took the list from me. "Where are we going to get helium gas?"

I shrugged.

Georgie thought for a moment, then grinned and held a pointer finger high like he'd just come up with the perfect solution. "We could buy a whole bunch of already-filled balloons. You know, like those silvery decorated birthday balloons that are already filled with helium."

"I don't think birthday balloons will work," I said, looking over Georgie's shoulder. "Most of these have to be black . . . and heavy-duty."

"Black birthday balloons?" Granpa said from out in the hall. "You guys planning a party for Count Dracula?"

Adding Glenn to our team had worked well, so I said, "Granpa, how would you like to be our advisor? Georgie and I are on a secret mission and we need an expert like you. The code name is Plan It."

Granpa came into my bedroom. He was wearing pajamas and holding a smoke detector. "Plan It, you say. Hmm. Does it involve foreign spies?"

Georgie poked me in the side and whispered, "Spacemen."

"Yes," I said to Granpa.

"Does this secret mission involve moving under cover of darkness?" He spoke softly, like he was afraid foreign spies might be eavesdropping.

"Definitely," I responded, poking Georgie back.

"Is there a dangerous and beautiful female involved?"

I looked at Georgie. I wasn't going to answer that one.

"Um, kind of . . . I guess," Georgie finally admitted. Then he poked me hard and grinned. "Two of them."

"Then count me in!" Granpa announced. "Special Secret Agent Melvyn Bud Mack reporting for duty. What do you need from me?"

We showed him Glenn's list.

"I've got the wire in the basement," he said. "The rest . . . hardware store. Except for those black balloons. When do you need this stuff?"

"Tomorrow," I said.

"No problem, kiddo. Except I have to drive limos all today, so why don't you and Georgie take the day off from espionage. We've got time. We'll get your secret mission gear after dinner."

Then Granpa's voice switched to a whisper. "Here's twenty bucks. I'm treating you guys to a day at the movies. I'll clear it with your moms. Tell the theater manager—his name's Joey—that you're Bud Mack's grandkid. When he was a teenager, I taught him how to drive. He'll treat you right."

I think Georgie and I woke everyone in our house (and probably everyone on my entire block) with our whoops and yells! We had no idea what was playing at the theater, but who cares?!

We got to the theater at eleven a.m. After I told

Mr. Patrick (Joey) who I was, he started chattering about what a great guy Granpa was, and the rest of our day was amazing except for one thing. Here's everything that happened. I bet you'll be able to tell which is the bad thing.

1.   We got to watch every kid-rated movie at the eight-plex, and we only had to buy one admission ticket.

2.   For lunch we had hot dogs. (Seconds were free!)

3.   Mr. Patrick kept refilling our popcorn boxes whenever we wanted.

4.   The only thing we didn't get free was candy, but we were so full of popcorn, we only bought two treats each.

5.   Kandy was at the theater with a bunch of girls, and the first thing she said to me was, "Lana [giggle] told me you're hanging out at her house [giggle] tomorrow night [giggle-giggle]. I can't wait to see the two of you together at Diana's Halloween party."

When we staggered out of the theater, it was after five. We had watched four movies. My butt was sore from sitting so long. I hadn't thought once about our Massive Halloween Prank, but when I got home, I was ready for action.

Georgie and I eat lots of meals at each other's houses. We don't even have to ask. It's kind of a best-friend benefit. We mostly just show up and it's okay with our parents . . . unless there's a special meal or something.

Georgie used to live with only his dad. But now Ms. D (that's what everyone calls her at school) and her daughter, Joy, are living in Georgie's house. Ms. D is a hilarious lady, so I bet dinner-table conversation at the Sinkoff house is going to get much more interesting.

But it will never be as interesting as dinner at my house. Here's why:

1. Granpa has an opinion about everything. And it is almost always weird, different, loud . . . or all three.

2. My mom is very smart. When she says something it is always because she knows what she is talking about.

3. My dad reads a lot, so he has lots of facts

in his head. He uses these facts to argue with Granpa, which almost always causes Granpa to change the subject and start talking about something else.

4. Goon either says something to get me upset or waits until Granpa pauses to chew and then chatters about her friends and ballet and her latest boyfriend. Because what she talks about is so boring to me, I try to get her totally agitated by nodding like I'm sooooo very interested or yawning like I'm totally bored.

5. I ask tons of questions and laugh a lot. (If Georgie's eating with us, he laughs, too.)

And you never know what might get a Mack Family dinnertime conversation started.

We were about halfway through the meal (I wasn't eating very much because of all the popcorn) when Goon said, "Pass me the mashed potatoes, please."

Granpa picked up the bowl and held it high in the air. "Mashed potatoes! Everybody likes mashed potatoes. So next summer at camp, I'm going to get the campers to plant a vegetable garden. I know where

I can get seeds guaranteed to grow potatoes as big as your head."

"I don't believe it," Mom said, not even looking up from her plate.

Granpa was still holding the bowl, so Goon repeated politely, "Pass me the mashed potatoes, please."

My father looked across the table at Granpa. "Hardly anyone grows them from seed, Pop."

I remembered reading that somewhere, so I said, "Don't they grow new plants by planting chunks out of an old potato?"

"Sure they do," Granpa said, waving the bowl back and forth, "if they want old potatoes." His voice got louder. "I'm talking about something brand-new, not yesterday's lunch."

He finally handed me the potatoes. There was only about one portion left in the bowl. That's when a devious plan popped into my head. I was supposed to pass it to Georgie because he was sitting next to Goon, but instead I said, "Shortstop," and scooped up a smallish spoonful.

"Shortstop" is the Mack Family thing to say when you want some of what you're passing. (Dad told me it doesn't have anything to do with baseball. It's because you are *stopping* the food *short* of where it's finally going.) I glopped the spoonful of mash onto my plate. Then I handed the bowl to Georgie.

That's when my mother looked up and noticed Georgie had no potatoes left on his plate. "Please take some, Georgie," she said.

"What about me?" Goon whined. "I asked first."

"You could go halfsies with my sister," I suggested to Georgie. I knew this would make Goon go crazy.

"That's it," she said, slapping her fork onto the table and standing up. "I am sick and tired of having to share my miserable life in this terrible house with a twerpy little brother who spies on me and knocks me down and cheats me out of mashed potatoes."

Everyone stopped eating and stared at her.

"I wish I were an only child!" she screamed. Then she spun around and stomped up the stairs.

When Goon's bedroom door slammed and something fell down with a bang, Mom plopped her napkin on the table, stood up, and said, "That kind of behavior is totally unacceptable."

As Mom walked upstairs, Dad gave me a hard look.

"What's this all about, Cheesie?" he asked.

Here's what I told him:

1. FALSE—Her life is not miserable.

2. FALSE—Our house is not terrible.

3. TRUE—I am a twerpy little brother . . . from *her* point of view.

4. TRUE—I did spy on her with my periscope, which we all know she viciously destroyed.

5. FALSE—I did not knock her down. She tripped over her own feet.

6. TRUE (but ridiculous)—A spoonful of mashed potatoes caused her to lose her temper!

When I finished, Dad said, "Uh-huh," sighed loudly, and went back to eating.

"You leave. You grieve," Granpa said. "Georgie's eating these taters." He reached across the table, picked up the bowl, and plopped a glop onto Georgie's plate. He licked the serving spoon and set it back in the empty bowl.

Mom came downstairs holding Goon's cell phone. No one said anything, but I knew Goon had gotten another no-texting punishment. I gave myself four more points, increasing my lead to 752–725.

After dinner, like Granpa promised, we drove to the hardware store and bought a small tank of helium and the LED, which, if you're interested, is pronounced "el-ee-dee" and is a kind of superbright lightbulb. Then Granpa drove us about thirty miles to a store that specialized in Halloween supplies. That's where we found heavy-duty black balloons.

When we got home, Granpa carried our Plan It materials up to my room. He put the box down and rubbed his hands together. "Got a busy day tomorrow. I am hereby resigning from further Plan It secret-agent work. Let me know how your trickety-trick turns out."

Goon appeared in her doorway. "Secret-agent work? What trick?"

It's always a terrible idea to let Goon know anything about any of my undercover plans, so I didn't reply. I quickly moved the Plan It stuff out of sight and shut the door.

"Now that your sister knows we're up to something, you'd better be on high alert," Georgie warned.

Of course he was right . . . and if I'd followed his

advice, lots of bad things might not have happened.

* * * * *

At three o'clock on Sunday (we had to wait until Glenn returned from some kind of church thing), Georgie and I carried all our Plan It material over to his house.

"Sergeant Cheesie reporting for duty, sir," I said with a sharp salute when Glenn opened his door.

Georgie's salute was much sloppier. "And General Georgie, too."

"You can't be a general," I told him. "At least not yet. You may have invented Plan It, but right now, while we're setting everything up, Glenn's in charge."

Georgie immediately re-saluted. "Private last-class Georgie Peanut-Head Sinkoff present and accounted for, General Philips, Your Highness, sir."

Glenn, who is almost always serious, smiled. "General is too high up the chain of command for my participation in this secret operation. I think I'll be Lieutenant Kareem."

Right away I could tell Glenn was into the fun. Kareem is his middle name.

"Let's take everything to my garage," Glenn said.

"Is that an order, lieutenant?" Georgie asked, saluting one more time.

"That is an order, private," Glenn answered immediately. Now he was grinning.

Georgie and I picked up the boxes and marched to Glenn's garage.

Glenn is a very organized kid. He had already cleared off a table for us. Georgie set his box on the table and saluted again.

I put down my box and started to salute as well but stopped and shook my head. "I think that's enough army stuff, Georgie. Let's just get to work."

"Yes, sergeant," Georgie said . . . with another salute.

"No more saluting," I said, a bit more firmly.

"Yes, sergeant," Georgie said . . . and he saluted again!

I know Georgie really well. He would keep doing his aggravating salute routine forever if I kept doing my sergeant thing. There is only one thing that would break this pattern. I pretended to be looking at something on the other side of Glenn's garage and walked behind Georgie . . . then jumped on his back, screaming, "Get control of yourself, Ee-Gorg!"

I had become Dr. Frank N. Cheez, brilliant and warped scientist, and Georgie instantly became Ee-Gorg, my brainless creation. You probably remember these guys from my earlier books. Georgie and I invented them in third grade.

Georgie began grunting and moaning, his head flopping from side to side. "Master . . . master . . . Ee-Gorg head! Talk in head! Voice make Ee-Gorg move arm!"

He began saluting rapidly over and over. I grabbed his arm. The up-and-down movement almost threw me off his back.

"Professor Kareem! Quickly! Bring me the cross-calculating readjustment disruptor!" I yelled.

Glenn had seen me and Georgie play this game before, but he had never been invited to participate. For a second he was confused, then maybe a little shy, then he just plunged into our make-believe. His voice got high and squeaky, and he talked with a goofy accent.

"Ob kors. Yass. I hab ezakly whad yu-u need." He picked up the small tank of helium and rushed over.

"Fire one!" I shouted.

Glenn pretended to blast Georgie with the helium. Georgie staggered.

I held on tightly and whispered loudly into my monster's ear, "Breathe, my empty-headed friend! Obey me at once and breathe, for I am the great Dr. Frank N. Cheez. Bwa-ha-ha!"

Georgie grabbed his saluting arm with his other hand and took a deep breath. Then he let it out with a long sigh. "Ee-Gorg like breathing. Breathing good."

"Yass. Ob kors. Breezing vury goot," Glenn squeaked.

Then we all looked at each other and laughed.

When we recovered, Glenn asked, "How many bright balloons did you bring?"

"Lots. They're orange," I replied, holding up a big balloon.

Picture the kind of balloon kids have at parties. These were more than twice as big.

"Good. And black ones?"

"Even more . . . just like you had on your list."

"Georgie," Glenn said. "Blow up the orange ones. Then we'll tie them together with the string you brought."

I took a ball of kite string out of my box and handed it to Glenn. Meanwhile, Georgie puffed one balloon to full size and was starting to tie it.

Glenn laughed. "With helium . . . Ee-Gorg."

Georgie muttered, "Ee-Gorg very stupid." He pinched the balloon neck and let the air out with a long farting noise.

Using the helium tank was easy. Granpa had shown us how to slide balloons onto the nozzle and inflate them. In just a couple of minutes Georgie had filled four orange balloons. Then I tied them to the kite string and we walked outside.

"These balloons are going to be our locator buoy," Glenn explained.

If you live somewhere where there are lakes or harbors, you probably know what a buoy is. (Weird-looking word, huh? Not many words have a *u* in front of an *o*. It's pronounced "BOO-ee" in most of the USA, but some lobstermen in Gloucester say "BOY.")

Buoys are floating markers that tell boaters where to go and where not to go. Our balloon buoy was going to be a marker, but it wasn't going to get wet. It was going to float high above Glenn's garage and help us locate his house once we set the telescope up on the hillside at Lana's.

"The orange balloons need to be forty or fifty feet above my garage," Glenn said. "That'll be high enough for you to spot them above any trees. But the black ones, for tonight . . . they'll need to be exactly two hundred seven feet high. I've done the calculations."

You have probably been wondering what we were

going to do with the balloons and stuff. Here's how Plan It was going to work:

1. Georgie and I would take my dad's telescope to Lana's house and use it to spot the orange balloons floating above Glenn's house . . . without letting the girls know what we were doing.

2. I would carefully note the exact direction the telescope was pointing.

3. Once it got dark, Glenn would pull down the orange balloons and replace them with a bunch of black balloons on much longer strings—207 feet high! Hooked to those balloons would be the LED light attached to a very thin wire (the power cord), which dangled alongside the string . . . all the way back to the ground.

4. After the girls had seen enough shooting stars, I would secretly aim the telescope back to where the orange balloons had been, and then tilt it up to where I knew the black balloons had to be floating (they would be invisible in the night).

5. Then we would text Glenn a signal, and he would tap the dangling power-cord wire against the lantern battery in some kind of mathematical pattern. That would cause the LED to flash.

6. The girls would see the LED's flashing signal through the telescope and think it was a signal from some alien civilization.

7. Mission accomplished!

Plan It was a great plan.

Georgie held the orange balloons while I tied the other end of forty feet of kite string to an old back-yard jungle gym Glenn had used when he was little. Then I let go, and we watched the balloons float upward.

"We've gotta get moving," Georgie said.

I guess he was getting hungry, so I asked Glenn, "Can you get everything else ready?"

Glenn nodded, then saluted . . . which made Georgie salute three times . . . which made me punch Georgie.

"I'll inflate the black balloons and get the LED

and its wire all hooked up and ready to connect to the battery," Glenn said.

I was glad I had included him in our secret mission. He was really having fun. Maybe Plan It was originally a Great Idea from Georgie, but how to make it work had all come from Glenn.

"Come on," Georgie said. "I don't want to be late for Mrs. Shen's dinner."

Georgie *never* wants to be late when there's food involved. But this was special. We zipped back to my house, got Dad's telescope, and walked up the hill to Lana's. We could see the orange balloons floating above Glenn's house the whole way there.

Chapter 8

Chicken Feet, Pig Ears, and Duck Blood

Just as we arrived at Lana's house, a soccer ball came flying out of her backyard. It hit high up in a tree, dropped onto the grass, and began rolling across her front lawn.

Then Oddny's head came over the fence.

I don't mean her head came flying over the fence like the soccer ball! (If it had, I'm sure this book would end right here because I'd be totally grossed out!)

Her head just popped up and was, I am absolutely sure, entirely attached to her body.

"Get the ball!" she screeched.

Georgie was carrying the telescope, so I took off running.

"EEEEEK!"

Lana's hill is not really steep, so at first the soccer ball was just rolling slowly. But it had a head start, so I sprinted.

I zigged around Lana's mailbox. I zagged around her mom's rosebushes. The ball rolled off the sidewalk and into the gutter. It bounced a couple of times, caromed off a car bumper, and rolled across the street. The hill was a bit steeper there, so the ball began to pick up speed. I glanced left and right, tore across the road, and took off after it . . . down the other sidewalk, my feet flying.

The ball passed two houses, bounded across a driveway into someone's front yard, and smashed into a hedge . . . where it stopped.

What happened next has happened to every kid.

You know how when you're running downhill,

going so fast that it seems like your legs can't possibly move fast enough to stay underneath your body? That's what was happening to me. I hurtled past two houses, totally out of control!

I stumbrinted (stumble + sprinted) across the driveway, digging in my heels, trying to slow myself. Directly in front of me was the hedge that had stopped the soccer ball. I was approaching it at break-my-neck speed.

At the last second, I turned my body and tumblashed (tumble + smashed) into the hedge with my right shoulder. Lots of things broke: leafy branches, part of a fence, and something I think was a hummingbird feeder. I lay on the ground, catching my breath. I moved my arms and legs. Whew! None of the broken things were my bones, but my shoulder did sting a little.

I reached out for the soccer ball. It had a large sticky black blotch on one side. I was trying to figure out what it was when Oddny and Lana ran up to me.

"Oh my gosh, Cheesie! You're bleeding!" Lana wailed, pointing at my shoulder.

I lifted my arm and looked at my sleeve. It had a small rip and was a little bit bloody.

"It's nothing. I must've cut myself on a branch," I said, standing up. My injury did not look the least bit serious.

Some kids get all panicky about blood. Goon is one of them. The slightest scratch makes her start squealing like she's going to croak in about three seconds. Bleeding doesn't bother me. At my last checkup, I actually asked my pediatrician how much blood you'd have to lose before you'd die. He said it's a lot. No one bleeds to death from little scratches and scrapes. Then he told me I have B+ (bee-positive) type blood. When Goon found out her type was A+, she started bragging hers was A-plus, and that she got a better grade.

Bogus!

(I have a page on my website about blood types. It has a chart that lets you figure out what blood type you are likely to have . . . if you find out what your parents have. You should check it out when you finish reading this book.)

"Are you okay?" Georgie yelled from Lana's front yard, three houses up the hill.

I gave him a thumbs-up and handed the soccer ball to Oddny. "I think it's got tar or something on it."

"I think your shoes, too," Oddny noticed.

My soles were drippy black . . . just like the blotch on the ball. I walked over to the driveway. It was black and sticky and looked like it had just been repaired with tar or asphalt or something. You could see where my heels had made dents in the surface.

"You better let my mom put a bandage or something on your arm," Lana said.

I nodded and took a few steps back up the hill. My sneakers left smeary black marks on the sidewalk. "Wait a minute," I said to the girls, turning around. "I better do something first."

I pulled off my shoes (carefully), carried them up

to the front door, and knocked. I could've just walked back to Lana's house, but sometimes you know that the right thing to do is not exactly the easiest thing to do.

A man opened the door. He was huge . . . like a pro football player. Also, a football game was on his television. Granpa told me to look adults in the eye when I speak to them, so I took a deep breath, and that's what I did.

"Umm, my friend's soccer ball kind of rolled down the hill and across your lawn and I was chasing it. . . ." As I told him what happened, his eyes got wider, and finally he walked past me to his driveway and stared down at how my heel prints had messed up his repair work.

"Oh, no. I just finished this," he muttered.

"I crashed into your hedge, too," I added, pointing at the broken branches.

"My bird feeder, too?" he said, looking a little angry. But then he noticed my bloody shirt, and his face changed. "Are you okay?" he asked. "Where do you live?"

"He's visiting me," Lana said. "Hi, Mr. Feeney." She had been standing off to the side, so I guess he hadn't noticed her.

Mr. Feeney's upset face immediately brightened. "Well, if you're Lana's friend . . . that changes everything." He then asked my name, so I told him.

"So, Jee Zee . . ."

(That's how he pronounced it. I didn't correct him.)

". . . are you going to be at Lana's for another hour?" he asked.

I nodded.

"We're going to watch for shooting stars after it gets dark," Lana told him.

"The Orionids, huh? It's a good, clear night for it,"

Mr. Feeney said, looking up at the cloudless sky. He motioned to Oddny. "Let me have that ball. I've got solvent that'll clean off the tar. And those, too," he said, beckoning for my goopy shoes. "I'll put them on your porch," he told Lana.

Mr. Feeney opened the side door to his garage, but stopped and turned back to me. "A lot of kids would've stomped my driveway full of holes and run away. You've an honest streak in you, Jee Zee. I appreciate that."

As the girls and I walked back up the street, I could see Georgie had set up the telescope on Lana's upstairs balcony and was looking through it . . . directly at me. "I have discovered a new star!" he shouted.

"More like new tar!" I hollered back.

"You can see RLS from here," Georgie said, turning the telescope toward school.

"Oh, let me see," Oddny said excitedly, and we all ran into Lana's house and up to the balcony.

We looked at the RLS flagpole and the new construction where Georgie and I had found the "thingie." (If you didn't read my last book, *Cheesie*

Mack Is Not Exactly Famous, I'm not going to spoil it by saying anything else.) We took turns spotting places in Gloucester:

1.   The pointy top of City Hall.

2.   Georgie's house. Mine was mostly hidden behind another house and some leafless trees.

3.   Rocky Neck Elementary, our old school. The playground was empty except for one boy shooting baskets. When it was my turn to look, he was just standing there picking his nose!

4.   A Coast Guard boat cruising out of the harbor.

5.   Four orange balloons floating above Glenn's house.

Of course, I did not tell the girls about the orange balloons. And also of course, I secretly memorized the numbers on the telescope that told exactly which way it was pointing when I looked at those balloons. But the best thing we saw was . . .

6.   Oddny's father washing their car in their driveway.

She shouted, "Hi, Papa!" But of course he was more than a mile away, so he absolutely could not hear her.

Georgie looked through the eyepiece. "Oddny, call your father on your phone and ask him to wave to us up here!"

She grinned and dialed.

"He's reaching in his pocket," Georgie said, still peering through the telescope.

"*Ég er í húsi Lana er að horfa á þig í gegnum sjónauka. Veifa til mín,*" Oddny said in Icelandic into the phone.

(Icelandic has a couple of strange letters in its alphabet. You might think that *ð* and *þ* are some kind of *d* and *p*, but they are actually both different kinds of *th*. Weird, huh?)

"Omigosh!" Georgie screeched. "He's squirting his hose straight up in the air and doing a crazy dance."

I grabbed my phone and edged Georgie away from the telescope. "Oddny, ask your dad to do it again." I put the phone up to the eyepiece and snapped several pictures. Here's the best one.

"Time for dinner!" Mr. Shen called.

The aroma inside the house was fabulous!

Suddenly I was super hungry. When we were all seated in the dining room, Mr. Shen announced, "Tonight my wife, who is an excellent cook, has prepared a very special meal." He was smiling broadly. So were Lana and Oddny. "We will have traditional dishes. Real Chinese food. No sweet and sour pork. No cashew chicken. No wonton soup."

Georgie couldn't help himself. He said, "I like sweet and sour pork."

Mrs. Shen came in carrying a steaming bowl of white rice. She set it in the middle of the table and returned to the kitchen.

Mr. Shen spooned rice onto his plate and passed the bowl to Georgie. By the time it went around the table, Mrs. Shen had returned with two more bowls of food. They had lids, so we couldn't see what they were.

Georgie was excitedly clicking his chopsticks, but he stopped when Mrs. Shen set the first bowl on the table.

"This is my favorite," Mrs. Shen said. "Hot and spicy chicken feet."

What did she say? I looked at Georgie. When I saw

how wide his eyes were, I knew I had not misheard.

Mrs. Shen placed the second bowl on the table. "And this is a dish Lana asked for specially."

"You can call it salty oink," Lana said with a huge grin.

"Sounds delicious," Oddny said, nodding seriously.

"That's a funny name, sweetie," Mrs. Shen said to Lana. Then she looked at me. "Actually it's soy sauce pig ears."

"You will love it," Lana said, reaching for the bowl.

Georgie had shrunk into his chair so much, he seemed to be smaller than me.

"And I have also made seaweed and duck blood soup," Mrs. Shen said. "I'll go get it."

"You are both athletes, I know," Mr. Shen said to me and Georgie. "Duck blood soup is very good for strength and stamina."

"I like rice," Georgie said softly. He stuck his chopsticks awkwardly into the mound of rice on his plate and tried to pick some up, but all the grains fell back to his plate before they reached his mouth.

What am I going to do? I thought. I was a guest

in the Shens' home. That meant I absolutely had to take at least a "no thank you" portion of everything served. That's what my mother had taught me. There was no way out. I was going to have to eat chicken feet, pig ears, and duck blood soup. I took a deep breath. *I hope I can do this.*

Mrs. Shen returned with a large soup bowl. She set it down in front of Mr. Shen.

Georgie raised his hand like he was in school. "Um, Mrs. Shen. I am actually sort of allergic to chicken feet and—"

"TRICKED YOU!" Lana and Oddny shrieked. They uncovered the bowls. Inside were sweet and sour pork, cashew chicken, and wonton soup.

Dinner was delicious. Georgie was so relieved, he happily struggled with chopsticks until Mrs. Shen took pity on him and gave him a fork.

I had thirds. Georgie had . . . who knows?

And all through dinner a little snicker kept running through my mind. *Okay, the girls tricked me and Georgie . . . but they have no idea that when it gets dark, it will be Plan It time . . . and the trick will be on them!*

Chapter CCC

The Black Goo of Mount Tarofini

"What else can go wrong?" Mackron hissed through clenched teeth. The base of the mountain had seemed like a paradise: palm trees, brightly colored flowers, and a tropical breeze off the white sandy beach. But once he and his party began climbing the jagged, barren sides of the sleeping volcano, the expedition had become a hellish nightmare.

As a world-famous explorer, Mackron was more than ready for sharp rocks and biting insects as large as small birds. But nothing in his long experience had prepared him for the Black Goo of Tarofini Island.

The journey had started well enough. Zinkojo, the strongest of his equipment bearers, had laboriously lugged the telescope and other scientific gear up the mountain's steep sides. Mackron had paused at the top to scout the view when one of the female bearers accidentally dropped a round teakettle. It bounced past him, clanking loudly and falling crazily down toward the small lake inside the volcano. Without hesitation or thought, Mackron bounded down the lava rocks after it.

But it wasn't a lake. Instead, the teakettle sat in a swamp of thick black goo that smelled like a mixture of rotting sewage and something poisonously

chemical. Even worse, the goo appeared to be dissolv-
ing the leather of Mackron's boots.

Mackron shook his head and mumbled almost silently, "Disaster . . ."

* * * * *

After I wrote chapter BBB, I realized how much I
liked Mackron, my unlucky explorer, so I decided to
bring him back again. This time I was inspired by:

1. the soccer ball I chased.

2. Indonesia's kablooeyed Mount Tambora.

I actually showed this to Mrs. Wikowitz to get
her opinion. She gave me comments and encouraged
me to revise it several times, and it got better each
time. Every kid thinks rewriting is boring, but it's
just like practicing XC or piano. If you do it enough,
you get better.

Of course you know who Zinkojo and the female
bearers are. And once you remember that the big guy
whose tar-covered driveway I sort of messed up was
Mr. Feeney, you'll be able to guess why I named the
volcano Mount Tarofini.

Chapter 9

It Came From Outer Space

After dinner it wasn't yet dark enough to see the Orionid meteors, so Lana invited us to play Monopoly. Little did she know that I am super excellent at that game. I have not kept a numerical score like I do with the Point Battle, but I estimate that Georgie and I have played over two hundred games of Monopoly since third grade. And I have won at least 75 percent of them.

[Georgie here: Somebody is totally lying. I have won one hundred ninety-nine out of the two hundred games.]

(I am leaving that interruption in because Georgie is 100 percent right that "somebody is totally lying." You decide who.)

I have a lot of strategies for winning at Monopoly, but since this is not exactly a book on how to win at board games, I will just give you two very valuable tips that I learned from my father (he is a world-class Monopoly champ . . . he even beats me!):

1.   The orange properties and the red properties are the best. The reason is simple. When you leave Jail, those are the spaces you're most likely to land on . . . and players end up in Jail *a lot* because there are four different ways to get there (*Chance* or *Community Chest, Go to Jail* cards, *Go to Jail* square, and rolling doubles three times in a row).

2.   If you can get three or four railroads *early in the game* (before others have hotels), you can really make money. Railroads are not as valuable late in the game.

One hour later, Oddny was winning (using tip #2 above, even though I didn't tell it to her).

Georgie rolled the dice and landed on B&O Railroad, then glanced out the window. "It's dark outside."

"That will be two hundred dollars you cannot

afford," Oddny teased.

"It's meteor time!" Lana said brightly. "I'll save the game, and maybe we can finish it some other day."

"Sounds good to me," I said. I had the orange monopoly and was starting to add houses, so my chances of winning were good.

Georgie was losing badly, so I do not think it was an accident that when he stood up, he accidentally knocked the board off the table.

(Monopoly is my favorite board game. What's yours? You can tell me on my website.)

We were lucky with the weather. It was a cloudless October night and not too cold. Mr. Feeney had returned the soccer ball and my shoes, so I put the shoes on, and we went up to the balcony. At first the sky looked black, almost starless. Mr. Amato had warned us it would take about five minutes for our eyes to get used to the dark and not to look at streetlights or car headlights once we were ready to observe.

Mr. Amato was correct about our eyes. After a few minutes, stars began to appear where we had seen nothing previously.

Suddenly Lana shrieked, "Look!"

A thin white streak shot across the sky and was gone.

"I forgot to make a wish!" Lana wailed.

"You can still do it," Georgie said.

"Uh-uh." Lana shook her head. "I'm pretty sure you have to have the wish in your mind *before* you see the shooting star."

"Okay," I said. "Then we should all make up a wish now and get ready to shout 'I wish!' when we see the next one."

"But don't tell anyone what it is," Lana added.

So we all stood there on Lana's balcony, looking up at the Gloucester night sky, making wishes.

Nobody would ever guess what my wish was.

I wished that no one would ask me what my wish was so I wouldn't have to tell them that I wished that no one would ask me what my wish was so I wouldn't have to tell them that I wished that no one would ask me what my wish was so I wouldn't have to tell them that I wished that no one would ask me what my wish was so I wouldn't have to tell them that . . .

Suddenly another white line, shorter but brighter than the first one, zipped through the darkness above.

The four of us screamed "I wish!" almost simultaneously. Lana was first by a half of a quarter of a whisker.

We didn't see another meteor for a few minutes.

"I guess that's it for the Orionids," Georgie said. "Kind of boring."

"You give up too easily," Oddny said.

She was right. Over the next five minutes the light show was great! I think each of us said "ooh" or "aah" about a dozen times as lots of little chunks left behind by Halley's Comet burned into nothing in the earth's upper atmosphere. After a while I figured it was time to get ready to launch Plan It.

"I'm going to look at some planets," I said, walking to the telescope.

"Me too," Lana said, coming over to stand next to me . . . a little too close.

On Friday, Mr. Amato had given us advice about what to look for with the telescope:

1. The planets are the brightest objects in the night sky and are easy to find.

2. We would be starting too late to see Venus or Mercury. Because its orbit is close to the sun, Venus is only visible just after sun goes down or just before sunrise. In fact, some people call Venus the Evening Star or the Morning Star (but it's a planet!). And Mercury is way too close to the sun for kids to see with a regular telescope.

3. And Saturn, because of where it is in the sky this month, wouldn't come into view until way after midnight.

4. The other planets (Uranus and Neptune . . . Sorry, Pluto, you're not a planet anymore!) would be too dim for us to see with my dad's telescope.

So that left Mars (called the Red Planet because it actually does look a little bit reddish through the telescope) and Jupiter.

"Just saw a huge shooting star!" Oddny said

without lowering her eyes from the sky. "Wouldn't it be terrific if one of those just happened to fly down like a fireball and land right here at our feet?"

"If it does, I hope it's a small one," Lana responded.

"Good point," I said. "With a big one there'd be a gigantic explosion and a crater where your house used to be."

Georgie added, "And the headline in the newspaper would be, 'Four Stupid Kids Vaporized by Meteor Blast.'"

"That's awful!" Lana said. She pushed Georgie to emphasize her disgust.

Finally I got the telescope aimed at Jupiter. "Who wants to look at the biggest planet in our solar system?" I asked.

For the next few minutes we looked at Jupiter. We could see the red spot on its surface and the different-colored bands that go around it. And we saw dots of light that I bet were three of its four largest moons, so I guess the other one was in front of or behind the planet. (There's actually a drawing of these four moons on page thirteen of my first book. They were discovered by Galileo in 1610.) Then I re-aimed the telescope, and we took turns looking at Mars. It really does look sort of reddish.

After everyone but me had looked at the Red Planet, I pulled Georgie to the side and whispered, "Text Glenn to send up the black balloons and start signaling."

Georgie gave me a thumbs-up and started thumbing his phone.

When it was my turn at the telescope, I casually redirected it—using the positional information I had memorized before dinner (aiming at the orange balloons, remember?)—into the dark sky directly above Glenn's house. I tilted the telescope up because Glenn had told me the black balloons would be much higher in the sky. I peered into the eyepiece. Even though I knew I wouldn't be able to see the black balloons, I was positive they'd be there. Glenn is very dependable. And then . . .

Yes!

. . . a dim flashing light came into focus.

Awesome!

It looked exactly like what it was supposed to look like: a signal from a faraway civilization.

I stared into the telescope for a few more seconds and then said softly, "This is interesting."

"What is?" Oddny asked.

I kept my eye on the flashing signal. "I don't know . . . ," I mumbled. "Weird . . ."

Now the girls were really intrigued.

"What? What do you see?" Lana asked.

"May I have a look, please?" Oddny insisted politely.

"It's not moving, so it's not an airplane," I said as I gave my spot to Oddny.

She peered into the eyepiece. "I don't see anyth—Oh, yes. A blinking light." She looked up at me. "What is so weird about a blinking light?"

"Well, it's high up in the sky, so it's not from a window or a lighthouse or something on a faraway hill. And like I said, it's not an airplane."

Both Dad and Granpa are major-league tricksters, so I know a lot about fooling people. Granpa says the most important thing is to say as little as possible. Let the person you're tricking fill in all the blanks. Let them convince themselves.

"Maybe it's a helicopter," Lana suggested. Now

she was the one looking at the blinking light.

I didn't respond.

"Yeah, maybe," Oddny said, "but even a helicopter moves sometimes. Has it moved?"

"Not at all," Lana said.

"Let me have a turn," Georgie said.

The girls moved aside.

Georgie made it quick. After a few seconds, he turned to the girls and repeated my earlier comment. "Weird."

It was Oddny's turn again. She stared in silence until suddenly—"Hold on! I think I—Lana, go get a pen and paper. I think there's some kind of pattern in these blinks."

Excellent! Oddny is a very smart girl. I absolutely expected this.

Lana was back with pen and paper in a flash . . . and with a flashlight, too.

"I'm ready," she said.

Georgie and I kept quiet. The two girls were running things now.

"Okay," Oddny said, her eye glued to the telescope. "Seven blinks. Pause. Um . . . eleven blinks . . . long pause . . . now just two . . . then three . . . pause . . . five . . . now seven."

Oddny kept at it for a long time, with Lana writing everything down. Finally Lana said, "It's just repeating now. I think the long pause is the beginning of the pattern, so it goes two, three, five, seven, eleven. Five numbers, and then it repeats."

"Could be a zip code," Georgie offered. "They have five numbers."

Lana shook her head. "No. This has six digits: two, three, five, seven . . . that's four digits. And then eleven is two more digits."

Of course I knew what the pattern was, but like Granpa had advised, I kept quiet. I wanted the girls to fill in the blanks.

(Do you recognize the pattern? Make your guess . . . and then read on.)

"Except for the first one, they're all odd numbers. . . ." Oddny was thinking out loud.

"And each number is bigger than the one before," Lana added.

There was a long silence. Oddny still had her eye glued to the eyepiece. "Same pattern over and over," she said softly. "It must mean something."

No one talked for a while, so I figured it was time for a hint . . . but I had to be very careful. I decided it would be best to talk about what the pattern *wasn't* rather than what it *was*.

"Whatever it is would be easy to figure out if the numbers went upward like two, four, six, eight . . . or if they doubled like two, four, eight, sixteen. But these . . ." Then I just let my voice drift into silence so their minds could work.

"Yeah," Oddny said. "None of these numbers is a multiple of any of the others."

"That's it!" Lana shouted. "They're not multiples of anything. These are prime numbers. We studied them last year."

"I forget," Georgie said.

"A prime number is a whole number that you can divide evenly by only one and itself," I said. "Like two . . . or five . . . or seventeen. Now do you remember, Georgie?"

I asked him later. He hadn't really forgotten. He was acting. And he didn't look goofy. He was very convincing.

"Oh, yeah," he said. "But so what if this is a bunch of prime numbers? Why should it matter what the pattern is?"

Suddenly Oddny jumped back from the telescope and started bouncing up and down. "Oh my gosh! Oh my gosh! OH MY GOSH!" she squealed. "I know! I absolutely know what this is."

We all stared as she caught her breath.

"Remember what Glenn said about alien civilizations using math to communicate with us? That's what this is! Don't you get it? This is a signal from space. From extraterrestrials!"

There was a pause while that sunk in . . . and then the girls started screaming.

A split second later, Georgie and I screamed, too.

Plan It had worked!

"This is unbelievable!" Oddny jabbered. She was jumping around like a monkey, her hands flying every which way. "I knew it had to be true!" She spun around and pointed at me. "I told you! I told you they existed, but you didn't . . . Oh my gosh!"

Just to keep the prank going, I started jumping around, too . . . and Georgie quickly joined in.

Lana wasn't jumping around. She was excited . . .
but she was also thinking. "Hold it. No one is going to
believe us. We don't have any proof."

"I know what to do," I said quickly. "Oddny! Is
the pattern still going on?"

She looked into the telescope and then back at me.
"Yes!"

I pulled out my cell phone, selected movie mode,
and held it up to the eyepiece. "I hope this works."

After a minute (I counted one-Mississippi, two-Mississippi, all the way to sixty), I stopped recording. Then everyone leaned in to watch what I'd shot. It was a little blurry and a little shaky, but you could see stars (they flickered a bit) and one tiny dot of light that blinked on and off with the prime-number pattern.

"This is the thing best ever!" Oddny said. She was so excited, she couldn't get her words straight.

"Hold on," I cautioned. "We cannot go blabbing about this until we find out if it actually is what we think it is."

The girls were barely listening. They were back at the telescope, taking turns looking at what they thought were signals from aliens.

I mouthed "Glenn" to Georgie, then acted out sending a text while shaking my head. I needed Georgie to tell Glenn to stop signaling.

With her eye to the telescope, Lana asked, "How can we do that? Who can we ask?"

I pretended like I was thinking hard, then said, "How about we show this video to Mr. Amato tomorrow before school? And, Oddny, you should get to show it to him. You figured out what it was."

"Absolutely right," Georgie said. His phone was back in his pocket. He had sent the text.

"I agree," Lana said.

Oddny acted kind of shy but also very excited and proud. "Okay, I'll do it. But you guys come with me."

"It's gone," Lana blurted.

"What?" Oddny and I said simultaneously.

"The blinking. It just stopped," Lana said.

"NO!" Oddny wailed.

"It's okay," I said. "I have the video."

Oddny calmed down a bit but was still very excited. "One more thing. Mr. Amato and lots of scientists and astronomers are going to want to know where in the sky we saw it. Is there a compass or something on this telescope?"

I told you Oddny is really smart. I took the pen and paper from Lana and wrote down the telescope position numbers I had memorized. But of course, I pretended to read them off the gauges or scales or whatever they call them.

Mr. Shen called from inside, "Cheesie! Your father is on his way over to pick up you and Georgie."

Lana and Oddny each looked for the blinking light again.

"Darn," Lana muttered.

"Double darn," Oddny double muttered.

I packed up the telescope and went downstairs. A few minutes later my dad pulled into the Shens' driveway and popped the trunk. I put the telescope in and whispered to Georgie, "You and I—and don't forget Glenn—just pulled off the most Massive Halloween Prank . . ."

He pounded me on the back and shouted, ". . . in the history of the universe!"

Lana and Oddny waved from her porch. They had no idea what Georgie had been screaming about.

"Did you see any shooting stars?" Dad asked as we drove down the hill.

"Lots!" I replied. "And the girls were contacted by bizarre creatures from a faraway alien civilization."

Then Georgie and I laughed for about three blocks. I bet my dad thought we were lunatics.

Chapter 10

The Meanest Boy in the World

I climbed into bed, still goofy with anticipation of how great our prank was going to turn out. But when I woke up, I wasn't so confident. It was like there was another Cheesie inside me wondering if we had maybe pushed our ET trickery a little too far.

On the bike ride to school, I asked Georgie if he was worried.

"Nah!" he shouted over the rumble of a garbage truck. "It's gonna be great! I know Oddny. She'll laugh like crazy when we tell her how we tricked her."

(Have you ever tricked anyone? You can tell me about it on my website.)

The girls were waiting in the corridor outside

Mr. Amato's room when we arrived. Oddny was fidgeting and grinning. Lana was grinning and fidgeting.

"You've got your phone?" Oddny asked.

Dumb question. I pulled it out of my backpack and held it high.

"This is the greatest day, oh my gosh, of my whole life," Oddny continued, talking very rapidly. "I couldn't sleep all night. Remember we all made wishes on that shooting star? Well, I never told you what I wished for."

"She told me last night, so she's not lying," Lana interjected.

The girls looked at each other, laughed, and then couldn't help themselves. They hugged. Oddny was so excited, she actually spun around once.

"I wished that someday I would actually meet a being from another planet." Her voice got so high, it squeaked. "And last night, my wish came true almost!"

"Here he comes," Georgie announced.

Mr. Amato was walking toward us. Diana Mooney, Eddie Chapple, and a few other sixth graders were with him. Most were carrying their science projects.

(They weren't due yet, but some kids like to turn things in early, I guess.)

"Mr. Amato! Mr. Amato!" Oddny shouted. "Get ready for something amazing!"

He slid his key into the door lock. "I am always ready for something amazing," he replied with a broad smile. "What do you have?"

I handed Oddny my phone and whispered, "Just touch here when you're ready."

"What I have is"—she showed my phone to everyone and paused to build the suspense—"just about the most amazing discovery in the history of the world."

Now Mr. Amato was really paying attention. He let go of the doorknob and waited for Oddny to continue.

"Remember we were talking about searching for life on other planets?" She took a deep breath.

Mr. Amato nodded. All the other kids were very interested.

"Well, last night, when we were looking at shooting stars, we did it! We found it!"

Mr. Amato's eyes widened, but he didn't speak. Oddny held my phone out in front of him and pressed the Play triangle. All the other kids crowded around, trying to see. As the one-minute video played, Oddny explained everything in a loud and confident voice.

". . . and then there's seven—you can count the blinks—and then eleven. It's a sequence. Over and over. Prime numbers from outer space. An alien civilization using math to communicate with us."

"Unbelievable!" Diana whooshed when the video ended.

"You are going to be in all the papers!" Eddie said.

Oddny was so happy, her feet did a little shuffle dance.

"Who took this video?" Mr. Amato inquired.

"Cheesie," Oddny replied.

Mr. Amato glanced at me. I said nothing . . . only smiled a bit.

Oddny had more to say. "We were at Lana's house. We were looking through Cheesie's father's telescope. And we knew you'd want to know where we aimed it." She handed Mr. Amato the positional numbers I had written down.

Mr. Amato glanced at the paper, then rubbed his bald head. "Very interesting, Oddny. But there's one questionable aspect to your discovery. Namely, other than light from a star, there is nothing in outer space bright enough to be seen from Earth. Unless extra-terrestrials could cause a star to blink prime numbers—which I suggest is impossible—this blinking came from somewhere on our own planet."

Oddny looked confused.

Mr. Amato continued. "Something is not quite right. Who saw it first?"

Oddny's reply was almost a whisper. "Cheesie . . ."

Mr. Amato looked straight at me. "Hmmm . . . Cheesie, you say."

I looked at Georgie. This was the moment. He nodded very slightly.

"TRICKED YOU!" I screamed at Oddny and Lana.

"TRICKED YOU!" Georgie echoed.

Laughing uproariously, I blurted, "We called it Plan It. Get it? And Glenn helped."

Then I explained, talking very fast. I was having so much fun telling everyone how cleverly we had tricked Oddny and Lana, I did not notice that no one was laughing. In fact, no one was even smiling. That's because everyone else was looking at Oddny . . . who seemed like she was about to cry. Then she let out one big sob . . . and ran away.

I shut up immediately, and everything froze. Moments before, lots of kids had been moving up and down the corridor, but for an instant, all movement stopped. (Not really, but that's what it felt like to me.)

Then Lana gave me the angriest look I have ever seen on any sixth grader's face. "Ronald Mack, you are the meanest boy in the world!" She stared for a moment more, then spun around and ran after her friend.

Diana shook her head and ran after Lana.

"Whoa," Eddie said, backing away from me and Georgie like we had a massive case of cooties.

The bell for first period rang.

"I guess your Plan It prank was not the success you were hoping for, huh, boys?" Mr. Amato said. Then he walked into his room, leaving us alone in the corridor.

Chapter 11

Silent Treatment

Oddny was absent from CORE. So was Lana when class started, but she came in with an excuse slip just as Mrs. Wikowitz finished taking attendance. Lana sits in the first row. I'm in the second. She gave me an I-hate-you look as she took her seat. Then she didn't look at me again until we left for third-period science.

And that look was I-hate-you-double!

Lana is in all my classes. This was going to be a miserable day.

I had to talk to Georgie after CORE. In the hallway outside, I grabbed his shirt and groaned, "Everyone thinks we're jerks."

"Yeah, and it was my stupid idea," Georgie croaked. "I really thought Oddny would laugh."

Then he smacked himself in the forehead and said, "WRONG!"

"Talk to her in science," I suggested.

"I'll try," he muttered.

"See you at lunch," I said.

Georgie walked away with his shoulders slumped.

Lana stayed totally mad at me in science and math. And lunch was worse.

Much worse.

Normally lunch is a fun time because Georgie and I sit with our friends and jabber about everything and nothing and whatever.

But today absolutely nothing was funny.

As we got in line, Glenn sort of stomped over and whispered loudly, "I didn't have many friends before I agreed to help you trick the girls. Now I have *no* friends. Thanks for nothing."

Before I could say anything, he stomped off.

Lana and Oddny were sitting at our usual table. When Georgie and I got our food and walked over, Kandy looked up and said, "We'd like you to sit somewhere else."

"Nah," Georgie replied, setting down his tray. "Cheesie and I are sorry."

When there was no response, Georgie slid onto the bench. Immediately, all the girls (five of them!) moved to another table. I stood for a moment, holding my lunch tray, then walked over to their new table. Neither Lana nor Oddny would look at me.

"Look," I said, "Georgie and I didn't mean to hurt your feelings."

None of the girls responded.

"It was a joke," I explained.

Silence.

I gave up and turned to go back to our usual table, but Georgie was standing right next to me.

"This isn't fair," Georgie said. "We didn't go all silent treatment on you guys when you tricked us with chicken ears and duck noses, did we?"

"Get lost!" Kandy said sternly. "They are NOT going to talk to you two . . . EVER!"

"And you both are completely not invited to my party anymore," Diana added.

We went back to our table, and for the rest of

lunch, no one sat with us. Not even one of the boys.

Traitors!

Fifth-period music, sixth-period PE, and XC practice were all pretty miserable. Only the teachers and coaches spoke to us.

"I want to stop in the office," Georgie said to me as we changed back into our street clothes after sports practice.

"Talk to Ms. D?" I asked.

He nodded. In addition to being his new stepmother, she was also the school nurse. (Just reminding you, in case you forgot.)

Ms. D listened to Georgie's explanation and then said, "It's simple. You got yourself into this. Apologize."

"We tried. They won't even talk to us," he moaned.

She leaned back in her chair. "Well, Georgie. If friendship with Oddny"—she looked at me—"and Lana . . ."

I nodded without even thinking about it.

". . . is really important to you boys, I suggest waiting a few days to let things cool off. Then find a way to convince them that you are sincerely apologetic."

"Like what?" Georgie whined.

Ms. D shook her head. "That's for you to figure out. You're going to have to work hard on this one."

The silent treatment continued for a week . . . at least from the girls. Eddie, Josh, and a few other boys sort of forgot about it and treated us normally. But not Glenn. Even though he wasn't getting the silent treatment (probably because he has never been a prankster before), he wouldn't talk to us. I guess he felt really sorry for Oddny.

Even worse, we became sort of infamous at RLS. Kids tweeted and sent texts and posted all kinds of stuff about what we had done and how we were being shunned. It was weird. If it hadn't made us kind of sad to be the focus of so much bad feeling, it might have been fun to be the center of so much attention.

Even worstest (no such word, but you'll understand when you read further), Goon got into the act.

Here's a day-by-day list of Goon's nasty dinnertime zingers:

1. Monday: Mom asked, like always, "Anything happen at school today?" Goon shook her head, "Nope. Eighth grade was pretty peaceful. But Cheesie had a big day. Tell everyone whose feelings you hurt." I explained. Mom was kind of upset with me, but when she learned that Granpa had helped us with the balloons and LED and stuff, she turned the pressure onto him. "Sounds to me like those girls need a dose of sense-of-humor pills," Granpa grumbled. (Thanks, Granpa.)

2. Tuesday: Goon looked at me as if she cared and said, "It must be very difficult to be the only sixth grader everyone hates."

3. Wednesday: Goon pretended to be upset. "All I hear at school is Cheesie this and Cheesie that. That's all anyone talks about. It's almost like you're really popular. Too bad they're not saying nice things about you."

4. Thursday: Goon made a fake confession. "I admit I was upset that my little brother was going to be at my school. I mean, it is embarrassing and all that. But I'm not upset anymore. I just feel sorry for him."

5. Friday: Goon put on a sad face and lied, "The girl that Ronnie embarrassed is probably going to have to see a psychiatrist. One of her friends told me she is so depressed, she can't eat or sleep."

My mother kind of agreed with the advice Ms. D had given to Georgie. She said, "You have to take responsibility for your actions and how they affect others. This may be difficult, but I have confidence that you will find a way to apologize and repair the damage you caused."

My father had a slightly different way of looking at it. "I feel bad for you. I think you need to apologize. Girls are very complicated. Good luck!"

Granpa, as usual, had a strong opinion. "The way I see it, kiddo, you are up to your Adam's apple in quicksand with those girls. Now don't get me wrong; I'm not sorry I helped you with your prank. The prank was fine. You just misjudged who you sprang it on. With girls like that—believe me, I know—you are going to have to come up with something extra special. Something so surprising that they simply forget why they were mad in the first place."

I had no idea what that meant.

By the end of the week, it was so bad at RLS, Georgie told me, "I think I'm going to resign as class copresident. Nobody likes me anymore."

I told Georgie, "If there were another middle school in Gloucester, I think I'd transfer."

I knew Georgie didn't mean it. I didn't mean it, either. We both felt the same. It's no fun to be shunned.

What I didn't know was . . . it was going to get much worse.

Remember way back at the beginning of this book when I said this adventure was full of tricks? Well, the most evil person I knew (Goon) and the smartest (Glenn) were working on a big one they planned to pull on Georgie and me.

It was called . . .

Chapter 12

The Sinister Plot

by

Glenn K. Philips

Introduction: At the request of Ronald Mack ("Cheesie"), my sixth-grade classmate at Robert Louis Stevenson Middle School (RLS), I have prepared this description of the planning and execution of what came to be known as The Sinister Plot.

Who: The perpetrators of The Sinister Plot were June Mack and myself (in major roles) and Oddny Thorsdottir and Lana Shen (who were brought in as co-conspirators). The victims were Cheesie and his best friend, Georgie Sinkoff.

What: The Sinister Plot was a carefully planned

sequence of events designed to trick Cheesie and Georgie.

Where: In the skies above Gloucester, Massachusetts.

Why: To help Oddny and Lana get revenge for being tricked by a hoax known as Plan It.

How: Three days after Plan It backfired, June Mack, Cheesie's older sister, approached me. She and I are members of the RLS Academic Decathlon team, so I knew her to be intelligent. I was entirely unfamiar, however, with her expertise in skullduggery.

[Cheesie here! Glenn has an excellent vocabulary. This means "great skill in trickery."]

June asked how I felt as a result of the failure of Plan It. I told her I was quite upset about participating in a hoax that hurt Lana's and Oddny's feelings. She then offered me the opportunity to seek "payback" against the original creators of the hoax. I accepted and worked with her over the next few days to create and execute The Sinister Plot, which we kept entirely secret from the victims.

In order to preserve suspense for readers of this book, Cheesie has requested I give no further description of The Sinister Plot at this time.

Chapter 13

RAT Sandwich

Of course, Georgie and I had no idea that Goon and Glenn had teamed up against us.

* * * * *

Since the next day was Saturday, Georgie slept over. We didn't fall asleep right away. We were just too miserable.

The last thing I said was, "This was my worst week ever at school."

And the last thing Georgie said was, "Yeah, me too."

In the morning, just after breakfast, Georgie and I were still in a mopey mood. We were clearing our breakfast dishes and Goon was at the table, eating yogurt, when Mom walked into the kitchen, pulling on her coat.

"I've got a few errands to do," she announced. "I want all the first-floor outside windows washed. Whose turn is it? June? Ronald?"

"I did it last time," Goon answered quickly.

"Uh-uh," I countered. "She did not! It's her turn."

(I didn't actually remember whose turn it was, but I wasn't going to give in without a fight.)

"No way," Goon said loudly.

Mom held up a hand and the arguing paused. "I will be back around two. If the windows aren't done by then, both of you will be grounded for Halloween."

"Mom!" Goon whined.

"But it's her turn," I moaned.

"Figure it out between you," Mom said sweetly. "You are intelligent children. I am certain you can find a mutually satisfactory solution." Then she left.

Goon glared at me. I glared back.

Goon huffed. I huffed.

Goon called me a name. I said it back to her twice. (I am not proud of that. Now that I am writing about it, it seems like babyish behavior.)

"I am *not* doing those windows," Goon said with lots of emphasis on the *not*.

"Fine," I responded. "Then we'll both miss Halloween. I'm *happy* to miss Halloween."

I know that sounds like another babyish remark, but it was actually true. Here's why:

1. Since Plan It had exploded in our faces, neither Georgie nor I had any friends at school anymore.

2. We had been totally UN-invited to Diana Mooney's Halloween party. (And I wasn't all that excited about going to it anyway.)

3. So the only thing being grounded would force me to miss would be dressing up in Granpa's black widow spider costume and hanging from a tree in our front yard—which would've been cool, except Mom had already said no to that idea.

Goon marched upstairs to her room.

"I'll win," I explained to Georgie. "There's no way Goon is going to pass up the eighth-grade cool kids party she's been babbling about." I sort of sneered when I said "cool kids."

"If you get grounded, what am I going to do for Halloween without you?" Georgie said. "I could help you wash the win—"

I shook my head and yelled up the stairs, "We're going over to Georgie's to play video games! When you're finished with the windows, I'll help you put the buckets away!" As we walked into the backyard, I told Georgie, "She will definitely give in."

Georgie prefers action games where you run around like a commando, shooting guns and blowing up bad guys. I like games where you have to think before you act. Don't get me wrong—I like conquering the world, but I like doing it carefully, using both action *and* strategy.

At first I was so involved in the video game, I totally forgot about everything except conquering the world. But after a couple of hours, even though I was doing well (I controlled North and South America and almost all of Europe), our problems with Lana and Oddny kept interfering with my concentration.

"It's your turn," Georgie reminded me for about the tenth time.

"I don't think I can take another day of the silent treatment," I said.

"We'll come up with something. We always do,"

Georgie said. Unlike me, he was still totally focused on the game. His immense Mongol army had control of Australia, Africa, and most of Asia.

"It looks like we were going to have a showdown in Turkey," I said.

"Turkey!" Georgie said. "I'm hungry. Let's break for lunch."

We trotted through our backyards to my house. Goon was not washing the windows.

"Uh-oh. Bad news," Georgie muttered. He checked the time on his phone. It was nearly one o'clock. "Your mom's coming home in just over an hour."

"It'll be okay," I said confidently. "I know my sister. She will definitely give in." I opened the refrigerator. "How about a BLART sandwich?"

Remember those from my first book? Bacon, Lettuce, Avocado, Ranch dressing, and Tomato. Yum! But when I searched the refrigerator and couldn't find any lettuce, I made what I could and handed one of them to Georgie.

"Here's your BART sandwich, sir," I said, placing a plate in front of him just like a waiter in a restaurant.

"Looks more like a BRAT sandwich," Goon interjected. She had come down to make her own lunch.

By switching letters, Goon had actually done something funny (and maybe I'll call it a BRAT sandwich from now on), but I wasn't going to laugh. Instead, because she's a vegetarian, I said, "I could make one for you . . . and leave off the bacon. Then it would a RAT sandwich . . . which would suit you perfectly."

"Very funny," she muttered. She took a couple of hard-boiled eggs from a bowl in the refrigerator and made some egg salad.

After we had eaten in silence for a while, Goon said, "Mom's going to be home soon. Are you going to do those windows or not?"

I shook my head. "Nope."

Then we just stared at each other.

"Well, I don't want to get grounded or anything," she finally said, "so how about we have a contest to decide?"

"Like what?" I asked.

She opened the refrigerator and pointed at a carton of eggs. "How about an egg toss like we do at camp every summer? Me and Drew against you and Georgie. Whoever is farther apart without breaking their egg is the winner."

There was something very suspicious about her suggestion. She is a good dancer, which is actually very athletic, but she is definitely nowhere near excellent at throwing and catching.

I took a big drippy bite of my BART/BRAT sandwich. "What's the catch?" I burbled through the ranch dressing dribbling down my face.

"No catch. I just don't want to get Mom's punishment dropped on me for no reason. If I win, you wash the windows. If I lose fair and square, then that's that, and I wash."

Georgie was poking me in the side like he wanted to say something. I ignored him.

"Why an egg toss?" I was totally suspicious. You would be, too, if you had a sister like Goon.

"Because I'm eating eggs, Dope-o . . . and I just thought of it!" she snapped.

It was weird. My sister had given me a totally guaranteed victory. Goon and I go to summer camp every year, and Georgie is always the champion egg tosser in our age group. And I'm pretty good, too. She would definitely lose.

(Is there some kind of camp-type game you're really good at? If so, you could tell me about it on my website.)

"Okay. I'll accept your challenge," I said. "When and where?"

"In the backyard as soon as Drew gets here. I'll text him to hurry."

Ten minutes later the four of us were in the backyard, ready to start. I had Granpa's tape measure. Goon held out the carton of eggs and opened it. There were ten. "I'll take this one." She picked up an egg, then put it back and took another. "No. This one."

I examined each of the remaining nine eggs for cracks. It would be exactly like Goon to purposely crack a few and then hope I would choose one of those. Nope. They were all in perfect shape. Finally I took one from the middle of the carton and set the box down on our picnic table.

"We'll go first," Goon said.

"Camp rules?" I asked.

Goon nodded, and then moved about four feet away from Drew.

"Ready?" she asked.

Drew nodded. She moved her arm back and forth a few times and gently tossed the egg. Four feet is really close. Drew caught it easily.

"Your turn," Goon said.

"I'll throw first," I told Georgie. "Move back until I say stop."

Georgie stepped backward. When he was eight feet away, I called out, "Stop."

The secret to winning at egg toss is not how you throw. It's how you catch. It's easy to make a gentle toss. But when the egg flies through the air, the catcher has to have what Gumpy (my other grandfather who used to be a very good baseball player) calls *soft hands*. You don't just catch the egg. You cup your hands and move them downward as the egg reaches you, so that the egg makes a gradual and gentle stop. At Camp Windward, Georgie, like I said, is almost always one of the champions of egg toss. He has really soft hands. And if you drop the egg, the toss still counts . . . so long as it doesn't break. But it always breaks.

"Ready?" I asked.

Georgie rubbed his hands together. "Go for it."

I lobbed the egg. Georgie caught it easily. Now it was Drew's turn to throw to Goon. He moved even with Georgie and motioned for Goon to step a bit beyond where I was standing.

About ten feet, I thought.

Drew lofted the egg . . . and Goon caught it.

Now I stepped back, maybe two feet beyond Goon.

Georgie tossed the egg. I followed its motion through the air and began moving my hands downward as the egg reached the top of its arc and began falling. When it landed in my palms, it felt like a feather.

Then Goon threw to Drew. I used the tape measure for the first time: thirteen feet, one inch.

"Getting dangerous now," I taunted Goon as I moved backward another couple of feet. I tossed, and Georgie caught: fifteen feet, eleven inches.

Then Goon did something outrageous. "Enough fooling around," she said. "Let's make this interesting." She stepped backward and backward until she was about twice as far away as our last toss.

Stupid, I thought. There's no way.

"Hold it," I said. I was trying to keep from smiling. "Let me measure before you throw." I gave the end of the tape measure to Georgie. He held it to the ground at the toe of Drew's sneakers. I stretched it out until I got to Goon.

Thirty-three feet, ten inches. I chuckled to myself: *Impossible.*

"You are soon going to have egg on your face," I predicted politely.

"We'll see," Goon replied. She didn't seem worried.

If this story were some kind of reality TV show, now would be when you'd hear the music getting all jittery and excited. And just when you couldn't wait any longer, the station would cut to a commercial.

But this is Channel Cheesie. No commercials.

Drew moved his arm back . . . and with a big underhand movement, tossed the egg high in the air. I watched it go up, up, up. Drew had tossed it too hard and a little off target. Goon moved sideways and lifted her hands up by her face. Then the egg started down, down, down.

It's going to break! I thought. *My egg-on-the-face prediction is going to come true!*

The egg hit her upraised hands . . . but it didn't break. It actually bounced off them, up and away. Goon lurched forward, but it tumbled just out of her grasp. She stretched, grabbed, and as she fell, she caught the egg in her outstretched hands.

But then her elbows hit the ground . . . and the egg flew out of her hands . . . and hit the grass.

"Ha!" I shouted. "We win!" I threw my hands in the air and whooped!

But we hadn't.

Goon picked up the egg. It was whole.

"Measure me," she insisted with huge grin. "It's your turn."

I trudged over to her with the tape measure. Thirty-four feet exactly.

Georgie and I were in big trouble.

Chapter 14

Eggsplosion

I grabbed Georgie's arm and pulled him off to one side.

"What's the farthest you ever did an egg toss at camp?" I whispered.

"Not this far," he warned, gently rolling our egg back and forth in his hands.

I looked over at Goon and Drew. They were grinning.

"Wait a minute," I suddenly said to Goon. "Let me see your egg."

"Sure," she replied, holding it out in front of her.

I walked up to her. She grabbed my hand and placed the egg on my palm. Then she suddenly closed my fingers around it, crushing the shell.

Goo!

I wiped my hand on the grass and walked back to Georgie.

"We are in deep window-washing doo-doo," he muttered.

I grabbed Georgie's shoulders and shook them. "We can do this," I said. "Throw it to me straight . . . but not too high. Soft and straight. Got it?"

Georgie cleaned his glasses on his shirt, then smiled. "New Sinkoff world record coming up."

I unrolled the tape measure to thirty-four feet from where Georgie stood and then stepped back a bit farther and nodded. Georgie began rocking his right arm back and forth. I was completely confident his throw would be on target. I was not so confident of what would happen when the egg got to me.

Georgie's arm came forward, and he lofted the egg.

Goon hissed, "Loser."

Then the world went silent.

Not really, I'm sure. But I don't remember hearing any sound at all during the next few seconds. The egg, just a small white oval when it left Georgie's hand, grew larger against the blue sky as it came toward

me. It seemed to move in slow motion. Georgie's toss was perfect. I put out my hands. The egg dropped into them . . .

and exploded!

"Drew and I are going downtown!" Goon shouted gleefully. "Have fun with the windows." And she was gone.

Georgie picked a piece of eggshell off my chin.

Washing the windows took almost an hour. We finished just as Mom returned from her errands.

"Nice job," she said after a quick inspection. "What are those eggs doing out here?" She pointed to the carton Goon had left on the picnic table.

I picked it up. "I'll put them away." The lid was partially open. As I closed it, something didn't seem right, but for an instant I didn't know what it was. Then it hit me. Originally there were ten eggs in the box. Then Goon and I each took one. Now there were only seven. That didn't add up.

"Come with me, Georgie," I said angrily. "Something's fishy."

I marched into the kitchen with the carton of eggs and put it back in the fridge next to the bowl of hard-boiled eggs.

"What a sneaky weasel," I muttered under my breath.

"What're you talking about?" Georgie asked.

"My sister totally hosed us." I told him what she had done to win the egg toss.

(Can you guess how Goon tricked me? Think about it. If you can't figure it out, the answer is on page 160.)

It was a big Point Battle victory for her. She had caused me to do something embarrassing when others were around (four points), doubled because it was a really excellent embarrassment, and doubled again because she cheated and got away with it. I had to give her sixteen points. It was now 752–741. She was catching up.

Chapter 15

The Great Georgio and Mr. Big Ears

Sunday morning I was sitting at the picnic table in my backyard.

"Yesterday was terrible. Tomorrow at school will be worse. And then comes, I bet, the worst Halloween ever," I said to my dog.

(I talk to Deeb a lot. Even though she doesn't say much in return, it somehow makes me feel better.)

That's what I was doing when Georgie came through the won't-close gate into my backyard. Deeb instantly jumped up and began running back and forth between us.

One of the really great things about having a best friend is when you're down in the dumps, maybe he's not! Georgie was grinning. I stretched my arm out, palm down toward Deeb. Without a word, she stopped running every which way and sat at my feet. She is just about the world's greatest dog.

"I have another Great Idea!" he said.

"No, no, no!" I said, backing up a step. "You have been Mr. Loser-Times-Ten in the Great Ideas department."

"Okay, I agree," he said. "Maybe some of them haven't exactly worked out, but this one is surefire. Tomorrow at lunch, I dress in my Great Georgio outfit and do some fantastic magic for Oddny and Lana. I'll amaze and mystify them. Then we apologize, and they won't hate us."

Granpa had said we'd have to come up with something extra special. Something surprising. This was it!

"It's brilliant," I said.

"I knew you'd think it was a Great Idea!" Georgie

Answer: When Goon made her egg salad, she secretly placed one hard-boiled egg in the carton with the nine raw ones, for a total of ten eggs in the carton. Then she selected the hard-boiled one to throw back and forth. Obviously, I got a raw one. That left eight eggs in the carton. After I lost, she slipped Drew the hard-boiled egg, which he must have taken with him when they left, and exchanged it for a raw one he had sneakily taken from the carton. That's the one she crushed in my hand. That's why there were only seven eggs left. I'm sure that's what she did. But I can't prove it.

160

grabbed me by the wrists and swung me around until my feet flew off the ground, which caused Deeb to jump up and bark like a maniac.

"How about me? What do I do?" I screamed as I watched my backyard spin around.

"You're going to dress up as my assistant. Joy and Mom have a perfect costume for you. Joy wore it in a play when she was our age. C'mon!"

He dropped me and ran toward his house. I jumped up and sprinted, passing him on the way. I held his back door open. "Right this way, Mr. Great Georgio."

"Thank you very much, Mr. Big Ears."

You probably remember that my ears kind of stick out. But Georgie knows teasing me about them is useless because it doesn't bother me. *So what's with the Big Ears comment?* I wondered as I zipped into the house after him.

Well, I found out right away . . . and when I tell you what happened the next day at lunch, you're going to wonder about two things:

1. Why did I ever agree to do it?
2. Wasn't I embarrassed to death?

The answers are:

1. Because I was desperate.
2. Yes. Yes. YES!

So here's what happened. Monday morning was the same as the previous week. The sixth-grade girls (and some of the boys) continued the silent treatment, ignoring us like we were absent or invisible. At lunch we ate alone again, wolfing down our food in about three minutes and then dashing to the gym, where we had stored everything we were going to need for The Great Georgio Great Idea.

Because it was lunchtime, the gym was deserted. We took our costumes out of our lockers and put them on in a flash. Georgie was in an excellent mood. He looked terrific in his Great Georgio outfit (top hat, cape, coat, and bow tie).

"I am anticipating complete success," he said, setting down the small suitcase that contained his magic tricks and waving his magic wand in the air.

"I look ridiculous," I muttered.

"On the contrary, you look positively terrific," he replied, trying hard to keep from giggling.

I looked in the locker-room mirror and almost

choked. There I stood . . . Mr. Big Ears in a full-body
bunny rabbit costume!

Coach T walked by.

"We're practicing our Halloween costumes for tomorrow night, kind of," Georgie lied.

Coach T gave us a very strange look and went to
his office.

Two minutes later, after sneaking around behind
buildings, we were hiding behind the back door to
the lunchroom.

"I cannot believe I let you talk me into this," I
whispered.

"All you have to do is stand near me and do what
I say," Georgie said in a voice that was supposed to
be comforting.

"I am either very courageous or very stupid," I moaned.

Georgie peeked into the lunchroom. "Okay. Go!"

I picked up Georgie's small suitcase, took a deep breath, opened the door, and walked into the crowd of munching, chattering kids. At first no one noticed, but soon heads turned and kids started hooting. I paid no attention to the noise. I was totally focused on getting near the sixth-grade tables.

I stopped just a few feet away from Lana and Oddny. They were staring, openmouthed.

"Ladies and gentlemen," I called out like a circus ringmaster, "attention, please! For your pleasure and amazement . . ."

The room suddenly quieted down. Every kid and teacher was looking at me. The lunch ladies stopped serving.

". . . may I present, direct from command performances for the Queen of China and the Empress of Iceland, the most magical and mystifying magician the world has ever seen. The world-renowned . . . the sensational . . . the Grrrr-ate Geee-orgio!"

I flung my arm out toward the back door. Georgie

came striding into the lunchroom, waving his wand and blowing kisses to the screaming kids.

"Thank you. Thank you," Georgie said loudly. He bowed once, then extended his arm toward me. "Please give a round of applause for my assistant, winner of last year's carrot-eating contest, the fluffy pink-and-white Mr. Big Ears!"

The crowd went cuckoo bonkers!

I was so embarrassed. I'm sure my cheeks were as pink as my bunny ears. But I had a job to do, so I bowed, then peeked at the eighth-grade table. Goon was laughing so hard she was almost choking. If this didn't work, I would have to move to Australia and live with my aunt DeeDee.

The Great Georgio opened his suitcase, which unfolded instantly into a small table. Kids crowded in closer to get a better look. The Great Georgio raised his arms until the room was quiet.

"I shall begin with a most unusual feat of legerdemain."

(*LEH-jer-deh-MAIN* is a fancy word for magic.)

He continued, "Any ordinary magician can pull a rabbit out of a hat. I, however, will do a trick no other magician in the world has ever performed successfully. I, The Great Georgio, will pull a hat out of a rabbit!"

He quickly stuck his hand down the front of my rabbit suit and yanked out an RLS baseball cap.

It was so goofy, kids laughed and booed. Mostly laughed. The Great Georgio waved the cap in the air and then tossed it into the crowd. Lots of kids jumped to catch it. The Great Georgio raised his arms again and quieted the room.

"Watch closely," he said. "The real magic begins now."

In rapid succession and with lots of arm waving, the greatest magician in the history of the RLS lunch room:

1. performed several card tricks (one of which you can do because it is described at the end of this chapter).

2. made milk disappear from a glass perched on my outstretched palm.

3. used his magic wand to cause a red silk scarf to float back and forth above my ears.

After each trick, the crowd screamed and applauded. I snuck a glance at Lana and Oddny. They were watching intently . . . and grinning.

Finally, The Great Georgio held up his arms to show his hands were empty. Then he pinwheeled both arms until they were just a blur of motion . . . and suddenly stopped. In each hand was a bouquet of flowers. He walked through the sea of kids to Oddny and Lana and handed one to each, then took a deep bow and strode out the back door. The crowd screamed, stamped their feet, and pounded on the tables.

I folded up the suitcase. Then, laughing mostly at myself, I hop-hop-hopped out the door. Once outside, we high-fived in triumph and ran back to the gym to change.

Next period was music for me and Spanish for Georgie. But we were slow getting to class because tons of kids patted us on the backs or told us how much they liked the show.

"Your magic tricks were so totally excellent," Diana Mooney said to Georgie. "And you both are totally re-invited to my party." Then she reached up and pulled on one of my ears like I was still wearing my costume. "You looked so cute as a bunny rabbit." It was kind of embarrassing. And not because I have sticky-out ears.

Georgie does not get embarrassed by girls the way I do, but when we got to his Spanish classroom, Oddny was standing right in front of him, and she just stared and stared and finally said "Thank you, Georgie" in a very soft voice.

He blushed big-time.

When I walked into Mr. Noa's music room, my classmates began screaming, "Cheesie! Cheesie! Cheesie!" I stood near the doorway, sort of soaking it up, but then Lana jumped out of her chair and gave me a huge hug.

Total embarrassment! But I handled it because

now we were totally forgiven. I guess by being Mr. Big Ears in front of the whole school I had proved to the girls how serious I was about apologizing.

Mr. Noa, who had seen the magic show because he'd been on lunchroom duty, shook my hand. "Good job, man! Class act," he said.

Mr. Noa was born in American Samoa, which is an island in the South Pacific owned by the USA. (Go back to the map on page 14 if you want to know where it is.) I only have him one day a week, but he is amazing! He plays every instrument . . . at the same time! His one-man band includes a ukulele, a harmonica held up by a metal contraption around his neck, cymbals between his knees, a drum on his back hooked by a wire to one foot, a tambourine on the other foot, and a bunch of whistles and bicycle horns hung on his shoulders. When he plays, kids cheer.

Being congratulated by someone as talented as Mr. Noa kind of took away any remaining embarrassment I felt about the bunny costume and the hug.

We got more high fives in PE. And at the end of XC practice, even Glenn seemed to have gotten over

being mad at us. "Could you bring your father's tele-scope to Diana's party?" he asked.

"Sure. Why?" I responded.

"You two apologized by doing that magic show. I still need to make amends with Lana and Oddny, so I'm hoping to do it by supervising some real star-gazing at the party."

"No problem," I said. "Friends again?"

Glenn nodded, and we shook hands.

Little did I know that Glenn was hard at work on The Sinister Plot with my sinister sister.

The Great Georgio explains how to do one of his card tricks:

Remove any nine cards from an ordinary deck, shuffle them, and deal them facedown into three piles of three cards each. Ask someone to choose any pile, then show everyone the bottom card. Suppose the card you show is the five of hearts. Then make the three piles into one pile, being sure to place the chosen pile on top. Spell out loud F-I-V-E, dealing one card from the top of the pile facedown onto the table as you say each letter. Place the remaining cards on top of these cards and take up the whole packet. Now spell and deal facedown O-F, and again place the remaining cards on top of these two. Then do the same, spelling out and dealing H-E-A-R-T-S. Place the remaining cards on top as before.

Now pick up the packet and spell and say M-A-G-I-C, dealing the final card (the C) face up. It's the five of hearts!

This trick will work no matter which card you spell out!

Try it on your friends or family. They will be amazed!

—The Great Georgio

Chapter 16

Candy-Collecting Contest

The next day was Halloween. School was awesome! Georgie and I were finally out of the doghouse. Everyone liked us again.

At most schools, Halloween is a day when kids wear costumes. But the tradition at RLS is the exact opposite. Almost no kids dress up. The grown-ups wear costumes, and they do it big-time.

Principal Stotts came as a cowboy with chaps, boots, stirrups that clinked when he walked, and a ten-gallon hat. He strode up and down the corridors between classes, twirling a lariat. When he saw me and Georgie (we were almost late for first period), he shouted, "Git along, little dogies!"

Ms. D was a tall pill bottle with arms and legs.

The prescription label on her chest read: TAKE ONE HAPPY HIGH FIVE EVERY DAY. So she was slapping hands with everyone when we passed her.

Mrs. Wikowitz shocked everybody by dressing not in her usual black outfit, but instead as Glinda the Good in a huge pink dress, crown, wand, and lots of glitter. But once class started, she was all business, as usual. Some kids don't like Mrs. Wikowitz because she's really stern and super strict. But she knows everything about language arts and social studies, and if you pay attention, she makes every class interesting.

Mr. Amato looked like a huge oxygen atom. His body was the nucleus, and he had eight electrons (Ping-Pong balls on wires) orbiting around him. But he was not in his usual happy mood. Lana explained, "Remember he said his pet was missing?" That made me think about how sad I would be if Deeb ever got lost or dognapped.

Ms. Hammerbord, my math teacher, was dressed like a totally radical skater chick. She had torn-off jean shorts, her hair was dyed blue and red (RLS school colors), and she had a decorated skateboard.

Take one happy high five every day!

She held it up for everyone to see and bragged, "I got this bad boy when I was in seventh grade!"

Eddie Chapple blurted, "You act way too young to be a teacher. How old are you?"

Lana immediately whispered to me, "So rude."

Ms. Hammerbord never taught before this year, but let me tell you how cool she is. She jumped on her board and rolled right up to Eddie's desk. "That's a good question, Eddie."

But she didn't exactly answer him. She gave us a math problem instead.

"I am as old as the sum of the number of letters in the names of three states: the longest name, the shortest name, and the last state to join the Union."

So how old is Ms. Hammerbord? The answer is on the next page.

How old is Ms. Hammerbord?

Massachusetts, North Carolina, and South Carolina have the longest names (thirteen letters). Either Utah, Iowa, or Ohio would be the shortest (four letters). And Hawaii (six letters) was the fiftieth state. Therefore, Ms. Hammerbord is twenty-three (13 + 4 + 6).

But check this out! Glenn Philips got extra credit for proving that Ms. Hammerbord might be fifty-five years old because the official name of Rhode Island is The State of Rhode Island and Providence Plantations . . . and that has forty-five letters!

At lunch everyone was talking about Diana's Halloween party that night. Georgie had a bag of candy corn. He was sharing, but also even more . . . munching.

"What's the best costume you ever wore for trick-or-treating?" I asked the kids at my table.

"When I was little," Eddie bragged, "my dad made me knight's armor out of cardboard. He covered it with aluminum foil. It was totally better than store-bought junk."

"Cool," Georgie munched.

Diana laughed and said, "When I was in second

grade, every one of the eleven girls in my class came to school dressed as a princess!"

"Lame," Georgie munched.

"I had an unusual costume once," Josh remarked. "I guess I was about eight. My mom made me into a giant brown paper bag. The best thing was when I trick-or-treated, all I had to do was unfold the paper above my head, and people just dropped the candy in on top of me."

"Clever," Georgie munched.

"Most children don't celebrate Halloween in Iceland," Oddny explained. "We have Öskudagur. It's in February or March every year. That's when little kids dress up in costumes and hunt for candy."

"Interesting," Georgie munched.

(What's the best costume you ever wore? Please tell me on my Halloween costume webpage.)

"Well, I'm not trick-or-treating tonight," Eddie said.

"Me neither," Josh agreed.

Diana looked a little upset. "You are wearing costumes to my party, aren't you?"

Costumes? I thought. *We're supposed to have*

costumes tonight? I had totally forgotten that. I gave Georgie a questioning look. He shrugged.

"Yeah, sure," Eddie replied. "I've got a costume. But going house to house begging for candy . . . that's for second graders."

"You're probably not that good at it. That's why you don't like it," Georgie said with another candy-corn munch.

"What's that supposed to mean?" Eddie demanded.

"How about I challenge you"—Georgie was holding a handful of candy in the air above his mouth—"to a trick-or-treating contest?" He dropped candies one by one into his mouth.

Remember I told you how competitive Eddie is.

He immediately answered, "You're on!"

Six minutes later, after a lot of arguing and negotiating about rules, the Candy-Collecting Contest was all set. Except now it was teams. Eddie and Josh against Georgie and me.

The rules we agreed to were:

1. We start at 6:30 p.m. at Diana's house. The contest ends back there exactly at 8:30 p.m.

2. If a team is late, they give the other team one candy bar (of the other pair's choosing) for each minute late.

3. You have to go on foot as a team. No splitting up.

4. Straight trick-or-treating. No buying candy or accepting any from anyone else including from your own house.

5. No telling homeowners you're in a contest or asking for more candy.

6. The winner will be decided by weight of candy only (no apples, coins, etc.).

7. All-or-none prize. The winning team gets all the candy in the other team's bags.

To make sure nobody could cheat, we agreed that each team would be accompanied at all times by two girl referees who'd make sure everyone followed the rules. Diana and Kandy chose to go with Eddie and Josh. Oddny and Lana (now that they were our friends again) with us.

"We're going to be in costume, too," Diana stated firmly. "So the referees will be trick-or-treating at the same time as you guys."

"Okay with me," Georgie said.

"Yeah, whatever," Eddie added. "Just don't slow us down. Josh and I are going to be moving fast."

After XC and basketball practice we raced home. Georgie and I didn't have costumes, but we had an excellent plan.

Using nothing but stuff we had in our homes (and eating bowls of cereal for dinner because we had no time to spare), we worked hard until six o'clock that evening.

When we were finished, we had two pillowcases for our candy and the following junk for our costumes:

1. the head from my bunny costume

2. a small cardboard box painted and cut out to look like a television

3. a plastic pumpkin

4. a long coat

5. a sheet of construction paper rolled and taped into a long, thin cone

6. a paper bag with eye holes

7. two extra shirts for each of us

8. a roll of toilet paper

If you are wondering what our actual costumes were, you'll soon find out!

We piled everything into Georgie's red wagon and were loading it into Ms. D's car when my father came over with his telescope.

"Didn't you say you needed this at the party tonight?"

I smacked myself on the forehead. "Thanks, Dad."

Ms. D dropped us at Diana's at 6:24. In six minutes, our epic Candy-Collecting Contest would begin.

Georgie pulled the paper bag over his head, and I held the construction paper cone up to my face as a long, thin nose. We left the red wagon outside and carried the telescope to the door.

Diana's mother let us in. She took one look at us and asked, "What are you boys supposed to be?"

"I'm NOT Pinocchio," I said, grinning broadly. "But that's actually a lie." I pulled my paper nose away from my face. "Because if I told you the truth, then my nose wouldn't be this long."

When Mrs. Mooney laughed, she sounded just like Diana.

"And I'm the handsomest boy in the world," Georgie said from inside his paper bag. "If I don't wear this bag on my head, everyone will faint because of how good-looking I am."

"You boys are very creative," Mrs. Mooney said.

It looked like all the other kids were already there. Music was playing VERY LOUDLY! Kandy and Livia were dancing. Oddny and Lana waved to us. Georgie and I walked over to the food table. His paper bag mouth hole was too small, so he shoved some chips up through his neck.

"I thought you maybe weren't going to show up," Eddie said. He had drawn an S on his T-shirt and pinned a towel around his neck.

"What does the S stand for? Stupidman?" Georgie

said from inside his paper bag.

Eddie sneered, "Excellent costume, Sinkoff. You look better with it on."

"I'm not Pinocchio," I said, wiggling my cone nose. But Eddie didn't care.

Josh wore a camouflage shirt and pants. I guess he was supposed to be an army guy.

The girls were all wearing real costumes they had obviously spent a lot of time creating. Oddny was a Christmas elf with a pointy hat. Diana was a very colorful horse-racing jockey. Kandy was a striped candy cane (very cool). And Lana was Glinda the Good!

What?

"When I told Mrs. Wikowitz how much I liked her costume," Lana explained, "she said I could borrow everything. And then my mom sewed and pinned everything so it would fit me."

"You are such a teacher's pet," I teased.

"Get ready. One minute," Mrs. Mooney announced, looking at her watch. "Remember to be back by eight-thirty."

We all gathered on Diana's porch. A few of the

other kids were going trick-or-treating, but they weren't in any huge hurry.

"GO!" Mrs. Mooney shouted.

Eddie took off running, with Josh, Kandy, and

Diana following. Georgie and I pulled our wagon fast to keep up with them. Lana and Oddny ran with us.

There were lots of little kids in costume on the street, almost all of them with adults who waited on the sidewalk while the kids knocked on doors. We zoomed past all the walkers.

At the first house, we left our wagon on the sidewalk and ran up to the door. "Trick or treat!" we shouted . . . and candy dropped into all eight bags. Same at the second and third houses. But pulling the wagon was causing us to lag behind Eddie's team. They had left the fourth house (the one with the tar-covered driveway) when we arrived.

Mr. Feeney answered the door holding an immense bowl of candy bars.

"Excellent costumes," he said to the girls. "And what disreputable company you travel with," he joked, pointing to Cone Nose me and Paper Bag Georgie. It was obvious he didn't remember me.

Then he dropped three candy bars into each of our bags. It was triple what any other house had given us.

We ran back to our wagon.

"Operation Switcheroo," I called out.

"Huh?" Oddny said.

Moving at superspeed, Georgie yanked the paper bag off his face, pulled another shirt over the one he was wearing, and put the cardboard box on his head. I tossed my cone nose into the wagon, also changed shirts, and then put on the bunny head.

"Stay here and watch us," I said to the girls.

"What're you doing?" Lana asked.

"Going back to the gold mine for more treasure!" Georgie shouted as the two of us ran back up to the house. I jumped onto Georgie's back. He knocked.

"Trick or treat!" we shouted when Mr. Feeney reappeared.

"Well, well," Mr. Feeney said. He looked confused. "What are you two supposed to be?"

"I'm a TV," Georgie said from inside the box.

"And I'm a bunny on TV," I said.

Mr. Feeney laughed and dropped four more candy bars into each bag.

A few seconds later we were back at the wagon, changing once again. I switched to a different shirt, then began wrapping my head with toilet paper.

The girls started laughing. "Omigosh." Lana giggled.

Georgie put on the long coat and grabbed the plastic pumpkin. In a flash we were back at the front door. Georgie had buttoned the coat so his head was completely hidden inside it, and he was holding the pumpkin above the coat where a head was supposed to be.

"Trick or treat!" we shouted (this time with disguised voices . . . just in case).

Mr. Feeney laughed. "You must be a mummy," he said.

I nodded. (Mummies can't speak.)

"And who are you?" he asked Georgie.

"Jack O. Lantern," he replied from inside the coat.

As we ran back to the wagon, Georgie exclaimed,

"I couldn't exactly see, but I think this time he gave me six!"

Off we went to the next house, with Oddny shouting, "So clever. That is definitely *not* against the rules."

We trick-or-treated down the next block, using the switcheroo technique at the houses that gave out the most goodies.

"I just got a text from Kandy," Lana announced. "Eddie and Josh are running so fast, the girls can't keep up."

"Text her back it's against the rules," I replied as we trotted to another house. "If the referees aren't with them at all times, they're disqualified."

While Lana was texting, Oddny, Georgie, and I knocked on the door.

The woman who answered took one look at Georgie's paper-bag head and began scolding us. "Are you the boys who are taking candy from little children?"

"What?" I said from under my cone nose. "No!"

"Don't lie to me! Two boys who saw you do it were just here. They described you exactly. You should be ashamed."

I asked, "Was one of them dressed like Superm—?"

She shut the door in our faces. No candy for us.

We stomped back to where Lana was waiting with our wagon. "What a cheater Eddie is!" I exclaimed.

"There's nothing about it in the rules," Oddny explained.

"Maybe we better get to a different street," Georgie said.

"Good idea! C'mon!" I yelled. "This way." I took off running through a small park. The girls followed, with Georgie coming up last, pulling our wagon.

For the next half hour, unhindered by any of Eddie's tricks, we blasted through house after house, tripling up when the rewards were top-notch.

As the four of us passed in front of a three-story building, I got an idea. "Would you mind if we trick-or-treated inside?" I asked a lady who was exiting the lobby door.

"Of course not," she replied, and held the door open for us.

Bonus!

"Apartment building! Lots of doors close together!" Georgie shouted as we pulled our wagon inside.

Up one hall and down the next . . . we must've hit thirty apartments in less than twenty minutes. Our pillowcases were bulging when we exited.

After running to a few more houses, Oddny said, "Ow! I've got a stitch in my side. You guys go ahead. I'll catch up when you slow down to do another switcheroo. Okay?"

Lana looked at Oddny. "Really?"

Oddny nodded rapidly. "Go! I don't want to slow you down. As long as Lana's with you guys, it's still okay with the rules."

We were near Rocky Neck Elementary, my old school. I knew all these streets. "Okay," I told Oddny. "We'll just keep going straight. See you!" And we ran ahead.

Six houses later we got to 207 Eureka Avenue . . . The Haunted Toad, home of Ms. G. J. Prott.

There were lots of kids walking along the street, but none of them stopped at number 207. I think that's because The Haunted Toad looked haunted. (Duh!)

Georgie opened the gate, and the three of us went

up the walk and onto the porch. Georgie had on his paper bag. I had worn my mummy head for the last few houses. It was coming apart, and I was trailing toilet paper down my back. Lana wound me back up while I knocked loudly several times. Then we waited. (If you read my first book, *Cheesie Mack Is Not a Genius or Anything,* you probably remember that Ms. Prott moves very slowly.)

It took a long time for Ms. Prott to come to the door.

"Trick or treat!" we all said.

Ms. Prott is a very small woman with pure white hair and green-gray eyes. The most noticeable thing about her is the way she moves her hands. They are constantly in motion, flitting about like small birds. She stared at us, her eyes wide with curiosity.

Then I realized that with Georgie's paper bag and my mummy head, she couldn't possibly know who we were.

"It's me, Cheesie. And Georgie, too. And this is our friend Lana."

She instantly lit up. "Oh, my! How frightening and original you boys look. Your friend—what is your name again—that is a lovely costume. You look exactly like the good witch in *The Wizard of Oz*. Am I right? Am I wrong?"

"I'm Lana, and you're right," Lana said very softly.

"Oh, how I loved that movie. I saw it when it first came out. I believe it was before the war. Perhaps 1939. Oh, please . . . come inside," Ms. Prott said, waving a fluttery hand to beckon us.

"We're kind of in a hurry," I said. "We were at this other girl's party, and one of our school friends challeng—" Suddenly I realized I was about to tell her about the Candy-Collecting Contest, which was totally against the rules! So I clammed up.

"Everyone today is constantly in such a hurry," Ms. Prott said, her smile, just like always, switching on and off. "It must be a Halloween party. I always loved Halloween. My sister and I would dress up. As ghosts, usually. And we'd go on hayrides or bob for apples." She paused as if she were back inside that memory. "But I understand. These days it's hurry, hurry, hurry. That's this new century, isn't it?" She raised one finger. "I suppose you are trick-or-treating for candy. Am I right? Am I wrong?"

"You're right," Georgie replied.

"Yes," she said, turning away from the door to a bowl on a hall table. "You know it's almost eight o'clock, and you're the only children who've knocked on my door."

She began dividing the contents of her bowl of candy into three piles. "So why don't you three take all this candy. . . . I won't eat it."

Bonus!

Lana interrupted quietly, "Please . . . only one candy bar for me. The rest should go into Cheesie's and Georgie's bags."

Ms. Prott smiled at Lana. "Very well, young lady. I shall do precisely that."

Lana whispered to me, "If she gave me some, then I couldn't give it to you. But this way . . . not against the rules."

I gave her a huge grin. A few moments later, after Ms. Prott gave goodbye hugs to all three of us, we exited The Haunted Toad. Oddny was out front, waiting by our wagon. Georgie pulled a candy bar out of his bulging bag and dropped it into Oddny's. Lana chuckled.

"I can afford it," Georgie said.

I swung my bag of candy over my shoulder. "I bet there's almost three pounds in here."

Georgie hefted his bag up and down. "I think I have even more. I wonder how much Josh and Eddie have."

"I'll text Kandy and ask," Lana said.

One minute and one trick-or-treat later, Lana's phone buzzled (buzzed + whistled). "Kandy thinks they have just about four pounds. Both of them together."

"Just over a half hour to go . . . and we are killing them!" I shouted happily.

I had no idea that back at Diana's house, Goon and Glenn's Sinister Plot was waiting for me.

Chapter 17

A Creature Walks the Street

We were now only a few blocks from my house.

"Hey, Cheesie. Whatcha up to?"

It was Kevin Welch. He's a tall, blond eighth grader who used to be Goon's boyfriend and was my enemy in *Cheesie Mack Is Cool in a Duel,* my second book. When we became sort-of friends, Goon dumped him. Tonight, he wasn't wearing a costume.

"Georgie and I are in a trick-or-treating contest." (He wasn't giving out candy, so telling him wasn't breaking any rules.)

"Try my house," he said, pointing to a house across the street with a small Christmas-looking tree growing in the front yard. "Alex is still there. See ya."

We knocked on the Welches' door. Alex answered.

He was wearing his Little League uniform and a Batman cape.

"Do you like my costume?" he asked. "I'm a baseball bat."

"That's really funny," I said. And I meant it.

He gave us each a candy bar from a bowl of about twenty.

"That's the last one I'm giving out tonight," Alex said.

"Why? Are you going to eat the rest?" Georgie inquired.

"Nah. I'm going to my grandmother's. Kevin just told me to lock up and come on over."

"Yeah," I said. "We just saw him."

"Did you know it's bad luck if you don't give away all your Halloween candy?" Georgie said.

"Really?" Alex looked confused . . . which is pretty usual for him.

"Uh-huh," Georgie continued. "Maybe you better wait here for more trick-or-treaters."

"But I want to go to my grandmother's," Alex whined.

I knew what Georgie was doing. I whispered to

Lana, "He didn't ask for candy, so he's not breaking the rules."

"What're you whispering about?" Alex asked.

"Your candy," I said.

"I don't want bad luck," Alex said, then his mouth fell open. He was staring over my shoulder. I turned around to see what he was looking at.

A bunch of eighth graders were running around his front yard, wrapping the Christmas-looking tree with toilet paper. The ringleader was Drew Teague, Goon's so-called boyfriend. He hates Kevin. He and his pals were tossing TP rolls over every bush and shrub.

Alex pushed past me and waved excitedly. "Drew! Hey, Drew! Can I do it, too?"

Drew ignored Alex—which is pretty usual for Alex—and kept wrapping toilet paper around everything.

Normally I would have simply butted out. But Alex looked so sad, I sort of made something up that I thought would make him feel better.

"It's against the rules to TP your own house," I said.

Alex thought for a moment and then yelled, "Drew! I get it. But if you want to do this to your own house, please let me do it for you. Okay?"

Of course Drew ignored Alex. He wrapped toilet paper around the Welches' mailbox about twenty times, then took off running down the street with his buddies.

Georgie pointed at the bowl of candy, then shook his head sadly and let out a huge s . . . i . . . g . . . h. "What did I tell you, Alex . . . bad luck."

Alex stood for a moment, thinking hard (which from the look on his face must've hurt his brain). "I know what to do," he said suddenly. He grabbed the bowl and dumped all the candy into Georgie's bag.

"There! Now you have the bad luck."

"Unlucky me," Georgie said.

Alex closed and locked his front door, then trotted happily off to his grandmother's house.

"Where'd you leave the wagon?" I asked after we had walked back to the street.

"It was right there," Lana said, pointing to a place on the sidewalk where there was no wagon!

Georgie looked at me, and we both said simultaneously, "Drew!"

"We'll get it back," I said. "He'll definitely give it to Goon, and she'll try to figure out some way to use it to mess with us." I started walking to the next house. "We'll just have to be ready for whatever she tries to pull."

I did not realize her Sinister Plot would be sprung on us in less than an hour! And I absolutely did not expect what I saw next.

There, in the middle of the street, just ambling along in the glow of a streetlight, was a huge tortoise. I ran out to look at it, and the others followed.

"Look at the size of this guy!" Georgie shouted.

"Wow!" squealed Oddny.

"My Granpa told me weird things happen on Halloween. This might be one of the weirdest," I said, spreading my fingers across its back. From head to tail, the shell was almost twice as wide as my outstretched hand.

"Be careful!" Lana cautioned, keeping her distance. "It could bite off your thumb."

"It's not a snapping turtle. It's a tortoise," I said.

I knew what it was because of its shape, which I read about in fourth grade during a thundery day when we spent recess in the library. (I have a weird memory, don't I? Anyway, if you're interested, I put a page about turtles and tortoises on my website.)

Just then car headlights came toward us. I handed

Georgie my pillowcase of candy, quickly picked up the tortoise, and ran to the sidewalk. It pulled its head and legs inside its shell.

"Look," Lana commented. "It tucks its tail in sideways."

"So do I," Georgie said.

"You don't have a tail," Oddny said.

"You can't see it because I tuck it in sideways," Georgie said with a grin.

I set the tortoise down. It didn't move for almost a minute. Then it stretched out its neck and legs, looked around, and took off running.

I am totally kidding!

Actually, it began walking very, very, very slowly, exactly like you would expect a tortoise to do.

"It probably belongs to somebody in one of these houses," I said.

"How do you know it didn't just wander here from the wild?" Oddny asked.

"Because *this* is a desert tortoise, and the nearest desert is probably in California or Colorado or somewhere."

"Cheesie's right," Georgie said. "Look how slowly

he moves. He couldn't have traveled very far."

"How do you know it's a he?" Oddny asked.

"Bald head," Georgie joked. "And why did the tortoise cross the road?" he asked . . . then answered, "To get to its shelter. Get it? Shell-ter!"

Oddny shoved him.

The tortoise was now heading for the street again.

"We can't leave him . . . or her . . . or it," Lana said. "It'll get run over."

So I picked up the tortoise (it went back into its shell), and we went door to door, asking everyone at every nearby house.

But nope. The runaway reptile didn't belong to any of them . . . and no one knew anyone who had a pet tortoise. But strangely, everyone was fascinated by a kid in a toilet-paper-falling-down mummy face holding a reptile, and even though we were doing more tortoise-asking than trick-or-treating, we got lots more candy.

"Omigosh!" I shouted. "We forgot the contest deadline. We're running out of time! Let's stash this tortoise at my house and get going."

We ran. But not at full speed. You cannot run very

fast with a twelve-pound tortoise in your hands! (I weighed it later at my house.)

As we neared a corner, a crowd of trick-or-treaters stood waiting on the sidewalk. The line turned onto my street.

"What are all these kids doing?" Oddny asked.

Of course I knew. "You just watch," I told her. "Follow me!"

We scooted around the corner and down the sidewalk. The line ended at my front lawn, where my father (with the kid-sized black widow spider suit somehow attached to his back) was standing behind a long table covered with a row of Granpa's decorated plastic buckets. Ten of them overflowing with candy! As each kid came up to the table and said, "Trick-or-treat," Dad dropped one candy from each bucket into his or her bag.

I was wondering where Granpa was when I spotted Superman Eddie, with Army Guy Josh, Candy Cane Kandy, and Jockey Diana right behind.

"Georgie, look!" I shouted. "They're at the front of the line."

I tried to move through the crowd.

"Hey!" a kid yelled. "No cuts!"

"Back of the line!" shouted another.

"This is my house!" I yelled back. "I live here!"

The kids ahead of me obviously didn't believe me or didn't care. They completely blocked my progress. And I was afraid I might drop the tortoise if I tried to shove my way through the crowd.

"Of course I know you guys," I overheard Dad saying. "Friends of Cheesie's get extra special treatment."

I looked up. My father was dumping large handfuls of candy from each bucket into Eddie's bag.

"Dad!" I screamed.

He saw me, waved, then gave Josh extra candy, too.

"Too late," Georgie said into my ear.

Moments later, Eddie and Josh walked right past us. Their candy bags looked very fat.

"Hey, Cheesie," Eddie said. "Great trick-or-treating here, huh? But I checked with the referees. You and Georgie are absolutely forbidden to get any candy from your own houses."

Kandy looked at Oddny and Lana. "It's in the rules. Eddie's right."

Diana nodded agreement. "We didn't let Eddie get any candy from his house, either."

"Nice turtle," Josh said as they walked away quickly.

"It's a tortoise," I mumbled.

"This way!" Georgie shouted.

He and the girls had found a way through the line into my driveway. We ran to my back door. My mother was in the kitchen.

"Mom, I need a box," I said breathlessly.

"A box for what?" she said. She hadn't turned around because she was pouring hot water into a teacup. Then she saw the tortoise. "Where did you get *that*?" she asked loudly.

I expected her to be frightened (because she does get a little bit weird around mice and spiders), but she put the kettle back on the stove and reached out to touch the tortoise.

"I had a little turtle when I was your age. Actually three turtles. I called them Shilly, Shally, and Shelly," Mom said. "Wow! This fellow is huge."

"We found it in the street near my old school," I said. "It's got to be someone's pet."

"We're going to put signs up tomorrow," Lana said.

Just then Deeb came into the kitchen. She instantly realized (dogs have excellent noses) there was something new and different in the house. Here is my translation of Deeb's yips, jumps, and tail wagging.

"Whoa! I smell something strange! Hey! What's that? Lemme see it! Hold it lower! It stinks soooo good! Down here, please! Oh! Can I roll on top of it? Hey! How about I give it just one lick? C'mon! Puh-leese . . ."

I set the tortoise on the kitchen floor and pushed Deeb out the door into our yard. When I came back, Goon had come into the room. The tortoise had taken a couple of steps.

"That is the cutest thing ever!" Goon gushed. "Can we keep it? Mom, please? Look how it moves. I'm going to name it Lightning because it moves so fast." Then she laughed at her own joke.

"You're not naming anything," I said.

The commotion brought Granpa into the kitchen. He was zipping up his zombie costume. I guess he had come in from working his front lawn candy table to go to the bathroom. "What do we have here?"

"The kids found a turtle," Mom said.

"If that's a turtle," Granpa announced, "I'm an unkie's munkle. Nope. It's a desert tortoise."

"I told you," I said to no one in particular.

Granpa squatted down to take a closer look. "Last time I saw one of these was when I was working on a special project for the Army out in Nevada. Probably fifty years ago. It had to do with messages from outer space." He gave me a squinty-evil-eye, so I knew he was teasing me about the ET trouble I'd gotten myself into with the girls.

He continued, "I can't tell you anything else about my project, however. Top secret. More important, though . . . I've got a really fine recipe for cooking desert tortoise. They're tough and stringy—like I am—unless you know what you're doing. Mmm-mmm-mmm! Mighty fine eating." Then he gave me another squinty-evil-eye.

"We are *not* eating that tortoise," Goon said angrily.

"I need a box," I said, looking up at our kitchen clock. If we didn't make it back to Diana's in ten minutes, the Candy-Collecting Contest would end, and we'd be in candy-bar penalty overtime. "We're in a big hurry."

"Oh, yeah," Goon said. "They've got to get back to their party. Get a box, Granpa."

Why does she care about our getting back to the party? I wondered.

Granpa brought a wooden crate up from the basement, and we put the tortoise (not named Lightning!) into it.

"What do you intend to do with this reptile?" Granpa asked.

"Keep it until we find out who owns it, and tomorrow I'm going to ask Mr. Amato what to feed it. Can you give us a ride to Diana's?" I asked Mom.

"Uh-uh," Oddny said quickly. "That's against the rules. Remember? You have to go on foot."

"Right. Never mind," I said. Then the four of us sprinted out the back door, lugging our bags of candy.

About five blocks later, Georgie puffed, "We are going to be so late."

The Hortoise in the Sugar Forest

"We are going to be so late!" Little-Gee wailed.

"You are right!" Big-Chee wailed back.

The two elves had gone on a happy walk through the Sugar Forest.

They had picked chocolate bars off the candy-bar bushes. They had picked lollipops off the trees.

But the curvy, swervy path was very long.

Now they were far, far away from the Moon House.

"We are going to be so late for our Hallowelf party!" wailed Little-Gee.

"What can we do?" cried Big-Chee.

"We can help you," two girl elves called out. It was Big-Lan and Little-Odd. They were riding on the back of a hortoise.

Little-Gee and Big-Chee were so happy.

They jumped onto the hortoise's shell next to their two friends.

"Hold on tightly," warned Big-Lan. "Our hortoise runs as fast as lightning."

Then ZOOOOOOM! The hortoise sped through the Sugar Forest like lightning . . . which was not his name.

* * * * *

When I was really little, I used to love picture books. I guess most kids do.

So I wondered what it would be like to write one. Because almost everything in those books is happy and fun (that's the way I remember them), I decided to turn the end of our Candy-Collecting Contest into a tale of four happy elves in the wonderful Sugar Forest trying to get back to a party at Moon House (Diana Mooney's). Of course I had to include the tortoise we found, but because he's (I assume it's a he . . . who knows?) very fast in this story, I gave him the legs of a horse (horse + tortoise = hortoise). And I reversed the sizes of the elves because . . . well, just because.

The stories in picture books are usually very simple, and the illustrations are supposed to be for little kids. (Maybe you could read these pages to your little brother or sister, if you have one.)

I had fun writing this mini-chapter but think it's more fun to write complicated stories for kids near my age.

And you can probably guess why the tortoise's name is not Lightning.

Chapter 18

Egg Sinkers, Guts, and Brains

Diana was peering out the front window as we ran up to her house. She opened the door before we got there.

"You're five minutes late!" Eddie yelled, looking at the time on his cell phone. "Open up your bags and show me what I get to take from you, loser boys. One candy bar for each minute." He pointed at the floor. "Now dump it out and pay up."

Georgie and I emptied our bags onto the floor. The pile was immense. It reached up to the ceiling and spilled out the front door.

Just kidding.

But there was a lot of candy. Eddie and Josh

dropped onto their knees and dug through the pile, picking out the five penalty bars.

Josh took two. "I like these two best," he said.

"I'm grabbing three of the heaviest." Eddie smirked.

Once they were done, Georgie and I shoveled all our candy back into one bag.

"Where's your team's candy?" I asked Eddie.

He held up a bag and then dropped the penalty bars into it. "Time for a showdown," he said.

"I'll get our scale," Diana said.

I whispered to Georgie, "The lump of candy in their bag looks smaller than ours."

Georgie nodded and whispered back, "Yep. Way smaller. We're going to win."

When I did my research on Milk Duds for my website (featured in my second book, *Cheesie Mack Is Cool in a Duel*), I learned that most candy bars weigh between one and two ounces. So I did some math in my head. Assuming the ones we forfeited were mostly the heavier ones . . . five times two is ten ounces . . . maximum. Sixteen ounces in a pound. We probably gave away about a half pound of candy.

That's not much, I thought.

Diana returned and placed a digital scale on the floor. "Who goes first?"

"Let them," Georgie said.

"No problem," Eddie replied.

He handed their bag to Diana. She put it on the scale. "Nine pounds exactly," she said.

Our bag was definitely chubbier with candy than theirs. We were going to win.

Georgie handed our bag to Diana. She placed it on the scale. "Eight point two pounds," she said.

"We win!" Josh yelled.

"Woo-hoo!" Eddie shouted.

Georgie and I looked at each other in disbelief.

"Hand it over!" Eddie bellowed. "Hand it all over."

Diana started to give our bag to Eddie.

"Hold it," Georgie said. "I want to check what's in their bag. How do I know it's only candy in there?"

Smart move, Georgie, I thought.

"No problem," Eddie said. He knelt down, emptied

the pillowcase onto the floor, then picked up a box of Whoppers as he stood up.

"Search all you want," he said. He opened the box, shook a few malt balls into his hand, and held them out to me. "Want some? It's the only candy you're going to get tonight."

I ignored his offer. "Check it out, Georgie," I said. Their pile of candy looked smaller, but it had been nearly a pound heavier. It didn't make sense.

Georgie dropped to his knees and dug through the pile. After a while he said, "Nothing but candy. Except this." He held up a ripped clear plastic bag.

"Somebody must've dropped that into my bag," Eddie said quickly. He took the plastic bag from Georgie. "I'll throw it away."

"Let me see it," I said.

"What's the big deal? It's just garbage," Eddie said.

"If it's just garbage, then what's the big deal about showing it to me?" I countered.

Eddie slapped the plastic bag scrap into my outstretched hand. I examined it closely.

"What are Egg Sinkers?" I asked.

"I don't know," Eddie said. Then: "Oh, yeah. Some kind of candy. I ate 'em." He pulled another malt ball out of the box he was holding and ate it.

"I'll keep this," I said to Eddie, and shoved the plastic bag into my pocket.

Eddie looked nervous for a moment, then muttered, turning to Diana, "Hey, can I have what I won now?"

"It's time for the games," Mrs. Mooney said from the doorway. "Why don't you children come into the den?"

"I think Eddie did win," Diana said. She handed our bag of candy to Josh.

"Ha!" Eddie crowed.

As everyone headed into the den, I lagged behind, pulled out my phone, and did a quick search. Bingo!

"Hold up!" I shouted. I walked up to Eddie and snatched the box of Whoppers out of his hand. He grabbed at me, but I dodged him, dropped to one knee, and upended the surprisingly heavy box onto the rug. Out poured about a dozen malt balls and about three dozen hunks of metal shaped like small eggs.

"How'd these Egg Sinkers taste, Eddie?" I said loudly.

Eddie just shrugged as the other kids gathered around.

"I thought there was something fishy," I said. "And there was. I looked up Egg Sinkers." I held up my phone for everyone to see. "You use them to weigh down your fishing line. They're made out of lead, I think. I didn't know what they were called, but my grandfather and I used them when we went fishing."

"That is so cheating," Diana said, grabbing our bags back from Josh.

"Nah," Eddie said. "I wasn't going to keep their candy. I just wanted to see if someone would figure it out."

Doesn't that sound like a total lie? I was pretty

sure it was, but I just took our pillowcase of candy back from Diana and smiled. I even shook Eddie's hand when he handed over his team's bag and said, "Good going, Cheesie."

The rest of the party was fun. First we bobbed for apples. In case you don't know what that is, you float a bunch of apples in a bucket of water and try to grab them with your teeth. You can't use your hands. It's a really old-fashioned game.

* * * * *

I have just stopped writing this story to ask Granpa if he ever bobbed for apples. He was watching a football game.

"Sure, I did," he said.

"How old is it?" I asked.

He looked up at the ceiling like he was trying to remember.

"It started hundreds of years ago," he began, "when Sir Isaac Newton and his wife were sitting under an apple tree next to a pond. An apple fell on his head and then bounced into the pond. He just sat there thinking about what gravity was, but his wife was hungry, and since she'd just had her nails painted, the only way she could eat that delicious fruit was to—"

At this point in his absurd story, I gave him a squinty-evil-eye and said, "I read a biography of him, and he never had a wife."

He said, "Okay. If you want to believe some old book from the library more than your grandfather, that's your business."

He went back to the football game.

* * * * *

Next we had a guessing game where we tasted five different sodas blindfolded and wrote down what we thought the flavors were. Mrs. Mooney warned us in advance that they were not everyday sodas like lemon-lime or cola.

I guessed right on corn (tasty) and bacon (gross), but almost everyone got those two. The other flavors were buffalo wing, celery, and bubble gum.

Lots of kids got three correct. Glenn guessed all five! He won a bunch of the sodas to take home. Some of the sodas were so disgusting, I'm not sure it was a great prize.

The last game was a test of courage. Mr. Mooney

came up from the basement with two covered buckets.

"I just took these out of the refrigerator. One is filled with brains and the other with guts. You have to guess which is which."

We all put our blindfolds back on. Then, one by one, we stuck a hand into each bucket. Everyone knew it wasn't real, but even so, it was so slimy and cold and glurpy and disgusting almost everyone squealed or *ugh*ed or screamed or just yanked their hands out immediately. Then we took off the blindfolds, and Mr. Mooney showed us what his buckets actually contained.

Real cow brains and genuine cow guts he had gotten from a butcher shop!

That's when the screaming GOT REALLY LOUD!

Mr. Mooney had tricked everyone.

Little did I know that the biggest trick of the evening was yet to be played, one that would turn out to be bigger than our Massive Halloween Prank. And it would be played on Georgie and me!

Chapter 19

Signals from Outer Space

"Eww! Disgusting! Gross!" We were all lined up at the sinks in the kitchen and bathroom washing cow juice off our hands.

"I want everyone to use this soap and then this disinfectant," Mrs. Mooney insisted.

When we were all scrubbed and calmed down, Glenn asked, "Who wants to look at craters on the moon? I've set up Cheesie's telescope in the backyard."

Mr. Mooney turned off the lights that shone into the backyard, and we all went out onto Diana's deck. While we waited for our eyes to get accustomed to the dark, we told jokes and stories about ghosts and zombies and Halloween.

(If you know any spooky jokes, please go to my website and tell me.)

"I know something," Oddny said. "I know something funny about extraterrestr—"

Lana clamped a hand over her mouth.

"What?" Georgie asked.

"She doesn't know what she's talking about," Lana said. Then both girls giggled.

Glenn turned to the group. "I've got the telescope aimed at the crater on the moon where the astronauts first landed. You can look first," he said to Diana, "because your name is Mooney and this is your house."

Diana skipped up to the telescope and took a long look. Everyone had a turn. Or two. Or three. It was really fun.

Finally parents started arriving to pick up kids. Diana went inside to help her mom and dad clean up. Eventually only Lana, Oddny, Glenn, Georgie, and I were left.

I was lying back on a deck chair, staring up at the stars and daydreaming (what do you call daydreaming when it's nighttime?), waiting for Granpa to come for me and Georgie.

What if gravity reversed, I thought, *and I started falling upward toward the stars. It's so far to the nearest star . . . I would fall almost forever!*

I tried to imagine that weightless fall, and I was almost feeling like I was lifting upward out of my deck chair when I heard Glenn, Lana, and Oddny talking.

"My father just texted me," Glenn said. "He'll be a few minutes late, but he'll drive you both home."

"Thanks," Lana replied. "I'll text my mom."

"Regarding the Plan It hoax in which I participated," he said, "I am really sorry I caused you to be embarrassed."

"It's okay," Oddny said.

"I was upset at myself for getting involved," Glenn continued, "and I let that get in the way."

"It's okay," Oddny repeated.

There was a long pause. My eyes were shut, and I was floating a few inches above my deck chair (not really, but that's what I was imagining).

Then Oddny said, "It actually was a really clever trick you guys pulled on me. Cheesie told me using prime numbers was your idea."

"What prime numbers?" Glenn asked.

The blinking pattern, I said to myself.

"You know. The pattern you blinked with that light," Lana explained.

"Four isn't a prime number," Glenn explained.

"There was no four," Oddny said.

"Yes, there was," Glenn insisted. "I sent one, two, three, four. Then I repeated it over and over."

I stood up and interrupted, "That's not what we saw. It was two, three, five, seven, eleven. You know . . . prime numbers."

"He's right," Oddny agreed.

"Then you weren't looking at our balloon light," Glenn said. "I blinked one, two, three, four. That's all."

"No way," I said. "What else could we have been looking at? Signals sent by creatures from outer space?" I pretended to be scared and let loose one of my super-scary, soft-and-spooky howls. "Ow-hooo-eeeee." Then I grinned.

No one else even smiled.

"I'm entirely serious. You must've been looking at something else. Follow me," Glenn said.

"What's going on?" Georgie inquired as we

walked past him to the telescope. He was standing on the edge of the deck, tossing pebbles into the dark, listening for the splash that would let him know each time he hit the Mooneys' backyard pond.

"Do you remember the coordinates for aiming the telescope at my house?" Glenn asked me.

"Sure," I replied. I had memorized the numbers.

"There has to be something else blinking out there," Glenn suggested. "Re-aim it like you did last time."

I lined the telescope up like I had before.

"But we're at Diana's house instead of Lana's," Glenn said, "so let me adjust for that." He fiddled with the dials. "Okay, take a look."

I peered through the eyepiece. At first I didn't see anything clearly. The telescope wasn't focused.

"Cheesie!" Mrs. Mooney called from the back door. "Your grandpa just drove up."

I looked up from the eyepiece. "Please tell him I'm packing up the telescope and I'll be right there."

Georgie said, "We better go. Your grandfather can get kind of aggravated."

"Yeah. Okay," I said, stepping away from the

telescope to pick up the telescope case.

"I'll ask him to wait while you look," Lana said quickly. She ran into the house.

"I'm really curious about what the other blinking could be," Oddny said.

If Goon had said that, I would've been suspicious, but Lana and Oddny? Nope.

"My dad's almost here," Glenn said, looking at a text on his phone. "Come on." He motioned to Oddny. They walked into the house.

I peered into the telescope and turned the focus knob. The field of view suddenly filled with a fuzzy, blinking light. I couldn't tell what it was, it was still too blurry, so I turned the focus knob a little more.

The large, fuzzy blinking light shrank down as it came into focus. It was a small, intense blinking light. A light that was surrounded by—

Huh? What? I rubbed my eyes and looked again.

It was an actual, honest-to-goodness flying saucer! While I watched, it rotated slowly and moved slightly back and forth in my view. Right in the middle of the craft, the light was blinking. It flashed two times, then three, five . . .

Seven flashes would be next, but I couldn't wait. "Georgie! Come quick!" I said in a loud whisper. "Look at this!"

I pulled my eye away from the telescope and let Georgie look.

"Omigosh!" Georgie said. "What's going on? What is this?"

"Remember when we showed the first video to Mr. Amato?" I said. "He said the signal couldn't come from another planet or star, that would be too far away. To be real, it had to come from something on Earth—or just above it. That's what this is!"

I pulled out my phone and switched it to Movie mode. "I've got to get a video."

I shot a minute of video and was getting ready to watch it when Glenn and the girls came back outside.

"My dad had to run by the store first," he said. "Did you see anything?"

Before I could answer, Granpa appeared at the back door, flanked by Mrs. Mooney and Diana. "Why in the blue blazes are you two so dead-flat slow?" he bellowed.

"We just saw a flying saucer!" I responded quickly.

"Great," Granpa said. "Pack up your flying saucer. This minute!"

Lana, Oddny, and Glenn crowded around me.

Oddny asked, "You saw what?"

"Did you video it? Let us see it," Lana added.

I started to explain, but Granpa bellowed, "Step on it! I'm missing the end of game six of the World Series."

"Meet me at Mr. Amato's room first thing in the morning," I said as I slipped the telescope into its case and headed for the house. "You know, like last time. I'll show you then. You won't believe it!"

As I climbed into the backseat of Granpa's car, I pointed to my phone and whispered to Georgie, "This is big. Really big."

Georgie whispered back, "Oddny was right all along. She believed space people were real."

I nodded. Then we watched the video I had made. Awesome!

I had no idea I had been hoodwinkingly tricked by the perpetrators of The Sinister Plot!

Chapter 20

The Most Excellent Halloween Prank Of All Time

"How was your party?" Goon asked me the minute we got home.

I ignored her.

Mom was on the couch doing a crossword puzzle. The box with the tortoise in it was on the floor next to her.

"How was your party?" Goon repeated. She had obviously just come home from her party because she was dressed up and had way too much makeup on.

"Why do you want to know?" I responded. She is never interested in what I'm doing.

"You see?" she said to Mom. "I try to be nice and he gets all snotty."

I had no time for Goon. I was holding (in my phone) actual proof of extraterrestrial life!

"Try it again, June," Mom said. Then she looked at me. "This time be nice to your sister."

Goon took a deep breath and gave me the fakiest smile. "Pretty please, my wonderful little brother, how was your party tonight? Did anything interesting happen?"

There was no way I was going to let her be one of the first to know what we had seen. In fact, I decided to tell no one until we had shown Mr. Amato.

"Nope, nothing interesting," I said.

"It was just a party," Georgie said.

Goon spun around on one foot (she is an excellent ballet dancer), smiled an evil smile, and went up the stairs singing.

She's in a good mood, I thought. *Something's going on.*

Mom pointed at the tortoise. "No one's going to be home tomorrow, and I think it's cruel to leave this creature cooped up all day in a box. Is there someplace you can take it?"

"We'll bring it to school," I said. "We have to see

Mr. Amato first thing in the morning. He'll know what to do with it."

"Good idea. How did your candy contest turn out?" Mom asked.

"We won," I said. Then it hit me. We'd been so excited about the flying saucer, we'd forgotten to bring our winnings home. "We left all our candy at Diana's," I said to Georgie.

"Not all of it," Georgie said. He reached into his jacket pocket and pulled out six candy bars . . . including three of my favorites.

"What're those?" I asked.

"These," Georgie crowed, "are our emergency insurance stash."

"Huh?"

"I set them aside just in case we lost," he said.

"You took them out of our bag? What if we'd lost by an ounce or two?" I said.

"Then I'd say, 'Whoa! Wait a minute. I forgot to put these in.'" Georgie grinned. "This way we could've lost our candy and ate it, too."

* * * * *

In the morning, Ms. D drove us to school.

"You boys seem very excited this morning," she said.

"We actually—you won't believe it—we actually saw an actual flying saucer last night," Georgie told her.

"And I have a video to prove it!" I added.

"You realize, I hope, that lots of these unexplained UFO sightings are elaborate hoaxes," she cautioned.

"This is not a hoax," Georgie said. "I saw it. I know."

Omigosh, were we wrong!

"I believe you saw something all right, but remember . . . Oddny saw something, too. And you convinced her it was real." She parked in the nurse's spot in the school lot, turned around, and gave us a long look. "Check it out before you tell everyone. That's all I'm saying."

"That's what we're doing," Georgie replied. "We're going to see Mr. Amato right now."

We got out of the car with our backpacks and my phone . . . and the tortoise in its box. Georgie put his backpack on top of the box so no one could see in. We didn't want to stop for a lot of questions.

Glenn, Lana, Oddny, and Diana were standing outside Mrs. Wikowitz's CORE room.

"C'mon," I urged them as we zoomed by on the way to the stairs up to the second floor. "You have to see the video. It's amazing!"

That started the "Really? . . . No way! . . . Come with us!" chatter going, so by the time Georgie and I got to room 220 (science), there were a dozen sixth graders trailing behind us. Also, Goon and Drew. Normally I'd tell her to butt out, but this time I was glad she was going to be there. When everyone learned that Georgie and I had seen a real UFO, I'd be RLS's big cheese (funny, huh?) . . . and she'd be just another eighth grader.

Mr. Amato looked a bit surprised when the crowd entered his room.

"We need to show you something," I said. "Georgie and I saw a UFO."

"Is this a continuation of the last bit of trickery?" he asked.

"This is not a hoax," I said. I handed Mr. Amato my phone. "I took a video that proves it." My voice was confident and strong.

"Well, well, well," he said, hooking my phone up to the computer that operated his big screen. "Proof is a very important aspect of good science."

I then told him about the prime numbers and Glenn's one, two, three, four . . . and how that led us to reexamine the sky. "Show the video. You'll see."

Mr. Amato messed with my phone, and soon a flying saucer appeared on the screen. A few of the kids in the room went "ooh" and "oh" and "wow."

"That's it!" Georgie shouted. "That's what we saw."

(I have included a snapshot taken from my video on the previous page.)

Mr. Amato froze the video so he could study the image. "Very interesting," he said.

"I think this might be one of the biggest discoveries of the century," I said proudly.

"And we're not going to hog this or anything," Georgie continued. "We're going to take our video to Washington, DC, and show the president."

"Maybe you better look at this first," came Goon's voice from the doorway.

I turned. She and Drew were holding a three-foot model of a flying saucer. It looked *exactly* like the one frozen on Mr. Amato's screen.

I was speechless.

Then most of the kids started laughing.

I was hugely embarrassed.

Glenn stepped forward. "This is the final part of what your sister and I call The Sinister Plot. It was our way of seeking payback for tricking Oddny and Lana. We thought it would be an excellent lesson for you and Georgie. I built that model spaceship, hung it from black balloons at my house, and used the LED light just like before."

Oddny said, "Lana and I sort of participated in The Sinister Plot, too. We gave the signal for your sister——"

"I was at Glenn's house!" Goon shouted.

"——to tap out the prime-number sequence," Oddny said.

Everyone was staring at me and Georgie.

Here's what went through my mind:

1. We had been tricked.

2. It counted as a sixteen-point loss for me in the Point Battle. The score was now 757–752. I was behind again.

3. Lana and Oddny got payback . . . which was probably sort of fair.

4. It was just too bad that Georgie and I were the victims.

Georgie and I stared at each other. Being best friends means that sometimes you know exactly what the other person is thinking. He gave me a tiny nod.

"Well," I said, "what you guys did to me and

Georgie was sneaky, underhanded, and probably . . ."

I nodded to Georgie.

". . . the most amazingly excellent prank in the whole world and outer space!" he shouted.

I grabbed Georgie's hand and threw our arms into the air.

"You tricked us good!"

Chapter 21

Venus in a Shell

Oddny shook my hand and asked, "No hard feelings?" I nodded. Lana just stood next to Oddny, smiling at me.

Glenn and I shook hands. "You can keep the model if you want," he said.

"I'd really like that," I said. "I think I'll hang it from the ceiling in my bedroom."

"I think I may just give all the participants and victims of The Sinister Plot some extra credit in science," Mr. Amato announced.

"Bonus!" Georgie yelled.

There was a tap on my shoulder. It was Goon.

"I've got to get to class," she said, "but— Never mind." She turned to leave, then stopped and pulled me off to one side and whispered, "Look. You are the twerpiest little brother ever, and what I'm going to say right now doesn't change anything. But you surprised me. I thought you were going to explode or cry or go ballistic. But you didn't do any of those. You acted kind of, well, mature." She paused, then said, "Never mind. Forget everything I said." And she left.

Omigosh, I thought. *My sister was actually nice to me!*

The first bell rang, and everyone left but me and Georgie.

"May I leave the model here until school's out?" I asked Mr. Amato.

"Of course," Mr. Amato said. "Put it back there by—What's that box?"

"Oh, yeah!" Georgie said, picking up the tortoise-in-a-box. "Cheesie and I found this, and we're going to try to return it to whoever it belongs to, but we don't know what to feed it." He carried the box to Mr. Amato's desk.

Mr. Amato looked in the box and suddenly shouted happily, "Venus! You beautiful girl! Where ever did you find her?"

Chapter EEE

Happily Ever Afterword

An afterword is what an author writes after the story is over.

So . . .

This adventure is over and *everyone* is happy.

Mr. Amato is happy because his forty-one-year-old desert tortoise is back. She had been missing for five days. He told me Venus had been his pet since he was younger than I am now.

Eddie and Josh are happy because even though they cheated on the Candy-Collecting Contest, no one is mad at them.

Georgie is happy because his red wagon mysteriously reappeared on his porch. No one knows anything about how it got there. (Drew?)

Lana and Oddny are happy because everyone is friends again.

Goon is happy because when I told Mom that she was nice to me, Mom took Goon shopping for a new winter coat and a new dress and new shoes and a new ballet outfit, and I think I might puke.

And I am happy because I have finished this book, and lots of kids have been to my website and told me how much they liked my adventures. (If you feel like it, please visit and comment.)

I am sitting at my desk in my bedroom as I write this, looking up at the spaceship that hangs from my ceiling.

Here's what I'm wondering. . . . Will there be a sixth adventure?

Maybe.

Perhaps space aliens will come to Gloucester and whisk me away to another planet. Maybe that's

where my next adventure will take place.

Or maybe not.

Either way, thanks for reading.

Your Pal,

Ronald "Cheesie" Mack

Ronald "Cheesie" Mack (age 11 years and 4 months)

CheesieMack.com

After the Afterword

Website Links

1. Your invention idea. (page 4)

2. Do you like this book or not? (page 4)

3. Rules for the Point Battle. (page 14)

4. What are your family traditions? (page 16)

5. What is your earliest memory? (page 18)

6. Want to see some optical illusions? (page 26)

7. How to build a periscope. (page 45)

8. Favorite-ice-cream-flavor poll. (page 64)

9. Different blood types. (page 98)

10. What's your favorite board game?
    (page 112)

11. Have you ever tricked anyone? (page 127)

12. What's your favorite camp-type game?
    (page 150)

13. What was your best Halloween costume?
    (page 177)

Acknowledgments

Hugs, high fives, and hoorahs to the over 60,000 third, fourth, and fifth graders whose schools I have visited. Their laughter stays with me. Many thanks to my editor, Jim Thomas, who ever politely and even more firmly redirected my wayward words, and to my agent, Dan Lazar, who brought me back whenever I wandered off the path.

Ann . . . thanks for the unqualified support and unencumbered freedom to write these books.

 **STEVE COTLER**

is a retired Little League catcher who's also been a shoe salesman, telecom scientist, singer-songwriter, *Apollo 1* computer programmer, Hollywood screenwriter, Harvard Business School MBA, investment banker, and door-to-door egg man. He lives with his wife and writes in Sonoma County in Northern California's wine country. He thinks he is and always will be eleven years old.

 DOUGLAS HOLGATE

is the illustrator of many notorious series for kids, including Super Chicken Nugget Boy, Planet Tad, Zack Proton, Zinc Alloy, and Bike Rider. Slowly but surely he is putting together a new, all-ages graphic novel, *Clementine Hetherington and the Button-Forbes Race,* co-created with critically acclaimed comics writer Jen Breach. If the Internet is on your computer, so is Douglas at www.skullduggery.com.au.

Visit Cheesie online at CheesieMack.com.
Visit Steve at SteveCotler.com.